1/95

THE BOYS FROM
ST. PETRI

THE BOYS FROM ST. PETRI

BJARNE REUTER

TRANSLATED BY ANTHEA BELL

Dutton Children's Books

NEW YORK

Library of Congress Cataloging-in-Publication Data

Reuter, Bjarne B.
The boys from St. Petri/by Bjarne Reuter;
translated from the Danish by Anthea Bell. —1st American ed.
p.   cm.
Summary: In 1942, a group of young men begin a series of increasingly
dangerous protests against the German invaders of their Danish homeland.
ISBN 0-525-45121-8
1. Denmark—History—German occupation, 1940–1945—Juvenile fiction.
[1. Denmark—History—German occupation, 1940–1945—Fiction.
2. World War, 1939–1945—Denmark—Fiction.]   I. Title.
PZ7.R3259Bo 1994   [Fic]—dc20   93-24161   CIP AC

First published in the United States 1994 by Dutton Children's Books,
a division of Penguin Books USA Inc.
375 Hudson Street, New York, New York 10014

Originally entitled *Drengene fra Sankt Petri*
and published in 1991 by Gyldendal, Copenhagen, Denmark.

Designed by Amy Berniker
Printed in U.S.A.
First American Edition
1 3 5 7 9 10 8 6 4 2

ON TUESDAY MORNING, APRIL 9, 1940, the people of Denmark were awakened by the drone of German military planes flying low overhead. The planes were scattering leaflets proclaiming, in poorly written Danish, that the German army had come to protect Denmark and Norway from England. The British, the leaflets said, planned to make a battleground of those two Scandinavian countries, and therefore the German army was immediately taking over the important military installations in both.

So the flat little country of Denmark, only half the size of the state of Maine and with a population of less than four million, was occupied by the Nazis overnight. Hardly a shot had been fired.

Although the occupation was "peaceful" at first, the Danes were immediately conscious of their loss of freedom. Nazi soldiers were everywhere. Most people felt helpless and hopeless. In 1942, however, a group of boys in the city of Aalborg on the Jutland peninsula began harassing German soldiers. Secretly they carried out operations that verged on sabotage, and their activities sparked the beginning of a wider and more cohesive resistance movement. This book is fiction, but it is based on their true story.

First we grab old Göring
By his big fat calves.
Then we knock down Goebbels—
We don't do things by halves!
We'll dangle Hitler from a rope
And right beside him Ribbentrop:
Look how stupid, all in line,
One, two, three, four Nazi swine!

SUMMER

1 9 4 2

O N E

There were two things Lars hadn't told Gunnar. One was a sure thing, and he wanted it to come as a surprise. It would show the rest of them, once and for all, that though he might be the youngest, he wouldn't be a problem once the action started.

He smiled and leaned across his desk, looking out at the lush backyard of the rectory, where laundry flapped in the June breeze.

The other secret . . .

With a sinking sensation, he left his desk. It was nearly four o'clock. Soon the long shadow of the church tower would, like a finger being raised in reproof, pass across the lawn, the flagpole, and the garden. The other secret had to remain a secret. Forever, if necessary. Lars laid his palm on the smooth curved surface of his globe. It turned easily. Texas came to a stop between his third and fourth fingers. When the war was over, when borders could be crossed again and the world opened up, he was going to travel, buzzing everywhere like a bumblebee, drinking everything in.

The clock struck four. He knew his brother would be there in one minute, exactly as arranged.

"But every secret," whispered Lars to himself, "has its weak point."

He heard Gunnar's footsteps in the corridor, firm and measured. His big brother Gunnar—a natural leader, a born authority, nothing short of an angel. After summer vacation, Gunnar would be a senior in high school.

Lars had known Gunnar almost before knowing himself. He remembered Gunnar's face above the hammock one summer day when the family was in the garden drinking coffee. Lars had been taking a nap outdoors after lunch. When he opened his eyes, Gunnar's blissful moon face was there, his red-gold hair framing it like a halo. Like magic. Gunnar's eyes were half closed—out of sheer peace of mind, their father would say. There was nothing behind Gunnar's head but the sky, infinitely blue. For one brief moment Lars had thought Gunnar was flying.

They were only eighteen months apart, but Gunnar had been born grown-up, an angel from St. Petri Church, a blessing. He had taken Lars's hand and led him over to the garden table where the coffee was laid out.

It was a prewar movie Lars was now seeing in his mind,

4

with a sound track of quiet voices and the clink of china. Peace and safety. Birds taking dust baths, pigeons cooing in the church tower. Miles away from the economic depression, the tramp of boots, the German occupation. If two shadows were cast on this Danish paradise in conversation, they were unemployment and Stalin's Russia. There were homemade rolls on the table, with fluted blue china plates and cups arranged around the blue coffee pot. Gunnar the golden boy sat at the end of the table, his gaze trained on infinity. A little smile hovered around his mouth, and his eyes were veiled. He had locked heaven inside himself.

Now Gunnar took his time outside the door. He still had that old knack with time: Nothing could rush him.

He might be older now and taller than his parents, but he hadn't really changed. He was still the pride of the town, his family, and, not least, the rowing club. When he led the singing in school assemblies, a light shone around his head. And when, as a matter of course, he took the lead in the Christmas play, people went home talking about another Kaj Munk, the great Danish poet and dramatist, who was also a minister whose anti-Nazi sermons were presently circulating throughout Denmark.

Lars hadn't grown up in anyone's shadow: He had grown up in Gunnar's light.

I really do love him, Lars thought to himself, smiling.

He looked up as his brother knocked on the door and entered.

The meerschaum pipe in the corner of Gunnar's mouth was

both an heirloom and a status symbol. It was amber colored, curly as a ram's horn, and smelled like burned slippers. Their sainted grandfather, the Bishop of Viborg, had sucked on the wooden stem of that pipe all his adult life, and an unconfirmed rumor had it that the mouthpiece at least could be traced back to the early 1800s, to Steen Steensen Blicher, a poet born near Viborg. Gunnar claimed that Blicher's small discolored teeth had made the famous scratches on it. And in Gunnar's eyes, or rather Gunnar's mouth, that pipe became something unique, something sacred—a relic that imbued him with the spirit of his forebears. Their father, who suffered from one-third asthma and two-thirds hypochondria, had given it to Gunnar, passing it on like the baton in a relay race—or like a scepter.

"So there you sit," Gunnar said, sucking at the pipe.

"Well, yes, it *is* my room," muttered Lars, rolling his eyes.

Unfortunately, his irony was wasted on Gunnar. With the air of an expert, his brother gazed at the little engraving that hung on Lars's wall. It was of some clergyman or other from Ribe, whose resemblance to a Scottish highland sheep was the reason Lars had tacked the picture up. Gunnar looked at the man's holy expression and cleared his throat. Gunnar himself would never look like a clerical highland sheep, although it had been settled ages ago that after his senior year he would go to Copenhagen to study theology. So far as Lars was concerned, Gunnar might as well just send two years' worth of pipe cleaners to Copenhagen and enclose the messy residue from the bishop's pipe, which was regarded as something nearly as precious as the Dead Sea Scrolls.

"Well, as you know, it's entirely up to you," said Gunnar. He sounded friendly yet authoritative, like a doctor telling his patient: Personally I'd recommend the operation, but it's your decision.

"I want to do it, Gunnar," said Lars, emphasizing each word. "I really want to do it."

Gunnar gazed out the window. Their mother was sitting in the garden, mending one of her husband's shirts.

"Eight-fifteen this evening, then," he replied. "During vespers. Father's going to read the announcement for Ellen and Viggo, and among other things we'll be singing 'Now thank we all our God.' " He looked straight at Lars and added, "We'll take the peg out in the middle of the second verse."

Lars glanced down at the garden, where shadows now lay. Where the turmoil of war, as their mother put it, would never come.

Gunnar hummed the hymn. He sang considerably better than the sacristan, who could make himself heard all over the parish, and twice as well as his father, the minister, who always said by way of excuse, "That's how it sounds when you try mixing hymns with asthma."

Gunnar gave Lars a brief smile. "What do you weigh, little brother?"

"One hundred thirty-four pounds, doctor. One hundred thirty if I take off my wooden leg."

Gunnar opened the window. "I was only asking for your own sake."

Lars felt mildly annoyed by all this rigmarole. OK, so he *was* a bit nervous. He knew quite well that his weight might be a problem.

"We'll tie a rope around you," Gunnar added.

"I can hold it in my teeth."

Gunnar looked at him skeptically, then stretched and yawned.

Fine arms he has, thought Lars. An angel's arms.

"We'll have to take a vote, you know," said Gunnar. "Two votes, really."

"Yes, yes, I know, Gunnar." Lars groaned, seeing the other two in his mind's eye: Gunnar's friends Søren and Oluf. Oluf was also called Luffe, and sometimes Professor. Along with Gunnar, they formed the core of the town's legendary rowing eight. Lars was cox and steered the boat. Gunnar rowed stroke. They were one of the fastest eights in the whole country.

It was almost half past four. Gunnar closed the window.

He and Lars always closed the window at half past four, which was when one of the three German brass bands stationed locally started marching down Østergade, past the German headquarters and then around the town.

Still, the noise filtered through. There was a war on, after all.

Lars had tried to join earlier. He knew what Gunnar and the other two planned up there in the tower of St. Petri Church. People discussed it in town, talked about the tricks someone kept playing on the Wehrmacht, the occupying German forces. But that it was the minister's son who was, like a second Zorro, the leader—that was a sworn secret among the group.

The first time Lars had asked to join, Gunnar had told him he wasn't old enough.

The music was louder now. Sometimes three German soldiers stood in the marketplace and sang a three-part song. There were even people who stopped, smiled, and clapped when the soldiers were finished.

"This evening, then," said Gunnar. "We'll meet at seven-thirty."

Lars inspected the lines on the palm of his hand in a preoccupied way. Gunnar left, but then stuck his head back in the doorway. His face wore an odd expression. By and large Gunnar had just two expressions: the serious, responsible one that inspired confidence; and the open, friendly one.

"Hey, do you smell anything? Apart from the pipe, I mean." Gunnar bent his head so that Lars could get a whiff of his new hair cream.

"What on earth have you been wallowing in?"

Gunnar gave him a playful punch. "Well, when a man's taking his girlfriend out . . . ," he said in a fake Norwegian accent, then laughed and was off again.

Lars knew a Norwegian accent, in honor of the Norwegian resistance, was the latest craze among the three boys who met up in the church tower.

He lay back against the big footstool and looked up at the ceiling. He could hear his mother in the garden. She liked

music. "They can sing, too, you can't deny that," she sometimes said.

"Well, yes, they aren't actually shooting us just now,"
Rosen, the organist, would answer her. "On the other hand
it's sheer torture, having their heavy-handed notions of culture
inflicted on us every afternoon."

Lars really liked Rosen, who had lived with them in the
rectory as long as he could remember. Rosen sailed on an
even keel, as Lars's father put it. His organ playing had made
the church famous.

Rosen was always saying the oddest things, and not just
because he was half Swedish. He never said what you expected. Last year, for instance, Lars had asked, "Why did
you never get married, Rosen?"

Mother had given Lars a playful slap for his bad manners.

"Because I'd rather be in love forever," Rosen had replied.

Later, Lars discovered that Rosen did have a girlfriend,
in Germany. At least, she wrote him letters and sent him
little paintings, which he always framed neatly.

His father, his mother, and Rosen. They walked on the
earth, going about their business. Above them floated Gunnar,
the angel. If something did occasionally bring a frown to the
brows of these four good souls, it was always on account of
idiot Lars here in his little room: Lars, who said the wrong
thing and arrived late, who belched at his own confirmation
service, dropped the wafer, and spilled the Communion wine,
and who came home from school with bad grades. "Lars is
a good boy," the school principal had observed, "but he's
wild, Mrs. Balstrup, there's no denying he's wild."

Well, it was to be this evening. This evening he would become a member of the St. Petri Group. Back in April, Luffe had stolen a cap from a German drummer. That was the sort of thing the group did, stealing street signs and German license plates and caps from soldiers.

Two days later, Lars had handed Gunnar a similar cap, as proof that he was fit to join. He had stolen it in a café, but it was just as good as Luffe's. Gunnar almost flattened him. Of course Lars still wasn't allowed up in the church tower; but he knew they had quite a few German caps, flags, and pennants hanging there, and at least one license plate.

But now, only four hours to go. Just four hours. He clenched his fists. One hundred thirty-four pounds. How much did Luffe weigh? One hundred fifty at the most, so one thirty-four should be enough. He wished he knew how much that wretched chandelier weighed! It was an ancient, colossal contraption. Once upon a time, long before the Balstrup family had moved into the rectory, St. Petri had had a big, strong sexton. By all accounts, he was the only man who could lower the chandelier when new candles had to be put in. Since then, of course, a set of pulleys had been installed, so that even the sacristan's wife could change the candles now. But once when Gunnar was doing some other odd jobs in the church and the sacristy, he had tried replacing the candles in the chandelier from up in the loft, so he wouldn't need the pulleys. And when he and Søren founded their secret society as a resistance group on the Norwegian model, for an initiation test they had reintroduced the old method of holding up the chandelier, making poor old Luffe undergo it first. During a funeral service too.

Lars had been sitting with his mother and Gunnar's girl-friend, Irene, near the back of the church when the chandelier dropped a meter and a half, right in the middle of "Always Peaceful When You Pass." Little clouds of plaster had drifted down.

But Luffe had managed to haul the thing up again, and as the astonished congregation started in on the lines "Fight for all you hold dear! I'll fear not what men say," Gunnar rose to his feet and left, smiling mysteriously.

It was at that precise moment, in the fall of 1941, that Lars had sworn he would be one of them. Whatever it took. And now—now there were barely three hours to go. The German brass band seemed to have marched back to its barracks. Or maybe to the hotel. The best buildings in town had been taken over by the army. The swastika waved above Apothecary Square. Outside the little town hall there were German sentries, sandbags, and barking dogs. The Germans did exactly as they pleased; they even walked around town with some of the local girls. The townspeople had not lost their ability to adapt, however. As someone had said to Gunnar at the shoemaker's the other day: "Before the Germans came, this town was famous for two things—its fjord and its unemployment. They can't take away the fjord, but they've certainly taken away the unemployment!"

Gunnar had spit on the floor.

Lars began to study the lines on his palms again, leaning

against the footstool. Rosen claimed that everything was written in the palm of your hand.

There were two things Lars hadn't told Gunnar. Two very
different things. He was keeping one to himself right now,
and the other . . . well, the other he would keep secret forever.
It had nothing to do with war. The very opposite, as a matter
of fact.

T W O

Lars had a memory of the church loft from when he was little and they had moved into the rectory. From the time when Denmark was free and no one was worried about a man called Adolf Hitler. The loft was a huge space with a lot of narrow hallways, where a powerful odor of dry wood mingled with the acrid smell of whitewash. It was at the very top of the tower, above the belfry, with enormous arches, like the petrified backbones of prehistoric animals, braced against the outer walls.

The whole essence of the church, all the mystery of the old tower and its latent eeriness, emanated from that loft. You had to climb up a thousand steps, around and around and around again. No one could take you by surprise up there, which made it the perfect hideout. So far as Lars knew, there were only four keys to the heavy door. His father had one, and the other three were in the hands of the St. Petri Group.

The organ sounded special up here, Lars now discovered, as if the music were welling up from the bottom of the sea. He had been led up the stairs blindfolded. An unnecessary display, he thought, but that was how Søren wanted it. Gunnar was down in the church, where the service was under way. He always sat in the same place, and no doubt he was holding hands with Irene while he kept an eye on the time and the chandelier.

Meanwhile Søren had led Lars in and told him to sit on the floor with his legs stretched out. The blindfold finally came off. Down in the church they had begun the second hymn.

Lars avoided Søren's penetrating, questioning gaze. He was Gunnar's best friend, someone who gave the shell and its famous crew of eight everything he had.

The loft was even more impressive than Lars remembered. It was lit only by candles now; they lent a solemn, almost primitive look to the arches.

"It's like being in the belly of a whale," Lars remarked.

Søren frowned and looked at his watch.

There was a platform in the middle of the big central space, and a black oak table on the platform. A candlestick discolored with mold stood on the table. Candles lit in honor of my initiation test, Lars thought. Old hassocks and big old-fashioned trunks stood in dark corners. Then Lars caught sight of the Nazi flag draped like a tapestry over the door to the stairs. There was an almost reproving look to it. That was what this was all about, after all. That was their reason for being here.

Luffe entered the loft in his usual fashion. Lars wondered whether Luffe intended his foolish grin to hide his basic preoccupation. He was like someone who seldom sees the light of day: a shadowy person, a ghost whose youth had been given over to the laws of chemistry. His red, rabbity eyes looked perpetually amused, as if he had a sixth sense, an attitude toward ordinary life completely unlike everyone else's. A stranger might have thought him feebleminded, slow-witted. Nothing could have been further from the truth. His nickname—Professor—was no accident. According to Gunnar, school had nothing left to offer Luffe. So far as Lars knew, Luffe devoted his time to just two things: first, the St. Petri Group and his friendship with Søren and Gunnar; and second, his own inventions.

Luffe now tied a rope around Lars's waist and told him to hold on to it. For once, Luffe looked serious and absorbed —maybe because he was the only one who had experienced what was coming. The thick rope was fastened to a set of pulleys that held up the weight of the chandelier as it dangled above the congregation on a glistening steel cable.

Søren rose to his feet. He looked briefly and appraisingly at Lars, nodded, then took up his position near the pulleys, where the peg holding the whole pulley device in place projected into the room by two feet. Lars knew the tug on his arms would come when Søren slipped the peg out. The rest would be up to him. He'd be supporting the entire weight of the chandelier.

Luffe smiled reassuringly. Or was he simply amused? You never could tell with Luffe.

"How much does that thing weigh?" asked Lars, and was angry to hear the tremor in his voice.

Luffe's pale face broke into a large silent grin. He looked positively deranged as he said, "Oh, it will stretch your arms to double their length."

Down below they were singing: "Now thank we all our God, with hearts and hands and voices. . . ."

Lars thought he could hear Gunnar singing at the top of his lungs. Perhaps he was nervous and wanted to let off steam.

Søren looked at his watch. Luffe moved back a little. Lars's mouth suddenly felt terribly dry. If only he could have a drink of water. Suppose he couldn't hold the thing up? Suppose he was too weak, too thin, too lightweight . . . ?

Of course they'd never let the chandelier crash down on top of all the people. They'd help him; they'd put the peg back in. But afterward . . . afterward the shame of it would wash over him. The humiliation. And then what?

His measure taken and found wanting again. Oh, no, not this time! This time it mustn't happen.

Lars had visited Rosen and asked him to read his palm. Rosen had not been particularly willing. "This isn't the Danish Fortune-telling Office," he had said in his light accent.

He was wearing his Chinese silk dressing gown and his silly slippers with the bells on them.

"Oh, come on, Rosen, you can't fail a friend in need," said Lars, holding out his hand.

Reluctantly, Rosen had taken it.

"I don't see anything special, anything—well, dramatic. A number of interesting contradictions. Loyal yet disloyal: It isn't going to be easy for you. That's all I can say."

"Thanks a million, Mr. Rosen. I feel so much better now!"

But sarcasm was always wasted on the organist. And now the palms of Lars's hands were about to be put to a quite different test.

He listened to the singing. They were beginning the second verse. If only he wouldn't sweat so much. He clenched his teeth and saw Luffe nod to Søren, who slipped the peg out without so much as blinking.

Lars felt the sudden tug like a whipcrack in his upper arms. The pull of it settled into his shoulders and neck: nonstop agony. As if the rope, the steel cable, and the chandelier itself had decided to tear his arms off. But he held on. He'd hold on even if he slid right over to the opening in the floor and plunged down onto the congregation.

He struggled convulsively to get a foothold, but he could feel the rope burning the palms of his hands. The blood was hammering, thumping, knocking in his veins.

Then he heard Luffe's voice, dry and monotonous. "Swear to keep the rules I read out to you."

Gasping, Lars let out a little breath and slid forward another foot. Blue and yellow lightning flickered behind his eyelids.

"Swear that you will never accept Nazi Germany's invasion of Denmark."

Lars nodded vigorously and suddenly tasted blood in his mouth. Had it come from his nose?

"Swear that you will go into battle, proud and upright, to fight Hitler and all his evil practices."

Lars stared at the rope, sure that it was about to tear through his hands. "That's enough," he groaned. "For heaven's sake, Luffe!"

"And swear to be eternally loyal to the St. Petri Group and to keep your oath of secrecy."

Lars cried out. For a moment he felt that his eyeballs were popping out of his head. He saw Luffe and Søren through a kind of fog. They were certainly taking their time slipping the peg back in.

Down in the church, Rosen was improvising a little piece on the organ.

Lars collapsed. He lay flat on his back and listened to his body. My pulse must be over three hundred, he thought. I'll never be human again. Brutes. What was the big idea?

He suddenly felt a blackness grow inside him: black hatred for the others, for exposing him to this pointless suffering. But when he saw Gunnar up in the loft the next moment, Gunnar in his homemade suit, looking so distinguished, so —well, so pure and proud and innocent—Lars decided to keep his mouth shut. Relief, then exultation, gradually washed over him. Gunnar patted him on the back. It both hurt and felt good.

"Welcome to the St. Petri Group," said his brother quietly.

Father, Mother, and Rosen usually had sandwiches and coffee after a late church service; Lars, Gunnar, and Irene were

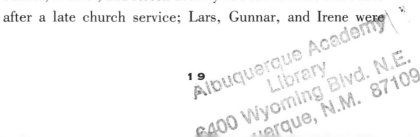

often there too. Irene gave the boys' mother a hand. She was already one of the family, a kind of daughter-in-law.

Gunnar was in the living room, talking to his father and Rosen about his exams. Lars was in the kitchen, where Irene was busy putting coffee cups on a tray.

"These are Danish," Father was saying. "I got them from the market gardener. They look good, they're reasonably priced—they just taste like burned slippers. Help yourself, Rosen. You can bite the end off for yourself."

He offered Rosen a cigar from the box.

Lars looked at Irene's back and wondered vaguely how much she knew. Maybe nothing. It would be just like Gunnar to tell her nothing.

With her back to him, Irene said, "Kirsten says you can tell fortunes."

Kirsten, who was in the same class as Lars, was friends with Irene. Lars knew Kirsten liked him, but it had never come to anything beyond a kiss or two under the viaduct as the train rushed by. She was a nice, sensible girl but, as he had confessed to Rosen one day in April, deadly dull. "Every time she opens her mouth I know exactly what she's going to say."

"That's right," said Lars casually. "One look at your hand and I know—I know everything!"

Irene threw him a doubtful glance and walked by with the tray. There was always a certain fragrance about her, a mixture of soap, new-mown grass, and French perfume. Never very strong. If he closed his eyes, he could evoke that scent and see images of the Middle East in his mind. The gateway to Asia, fat men with red fezzes, veiled women . . . adventure. Adventure and magic.

He saw himself too, in uniform. British uniform. Royal Air Force uniform. Why not? Once Lars had had a strange dream: He was running aimlessly through the dark city of Medina. Street traders sitting under brightly colored awnings stared out at him. They spit from toothless mouths. Lars ran on, from one woman to the next, ripping the veils from their faces. Where was she? At last, at last! He knew her by her fragrance, but suddenly he couldn't remove her veil.

In the living room, blue cigar smoke mingled with voices from the BBC broadcast. The politician and patriot Christmas Møller, who had recently fled from Nazi-occupied Denmark, was about to speak. It was good to know he was alive, sitting in front of a microphone over in England.

Lars wiped the kitchen table. Gunnar's black bicycle was propped outside the window. Maybe that was what started Lars thinking about the old, run-down café in the woods.

The rain had taken them entirely by surprise that day. It had come pouring down. They had cycled full tilt through the woods: Gunnar, Irene, and Lars. Irene's front tire got a flat, but Gunnar had his repair kit with him, as usual. They took shelter in the abandoned café. Last year's leaves lay on the bare floor. Gunnar went straight to work on the bike, while Irene tried to dry her hair with a sweater. Meanwhile Lars wandered around, looking at all the little windows and the little balustrades where the paint was peeling.

"What a pit!" exclaimed Gunnar, grinning at Irene, who had turned her back to Lars to wring the rainwater out of her blouse.

Lars discovered a small hallway where he imagined waiters used to run back and forth, carrying beer, cakes, and coffee cups. Outside the café, the grass was tall. It reminded him of the song they sang down by the fjord at songfests, about weed seeds drifting over hedges from someone else's yard. The song made everyone think of the unwelcome influence of Nazi Germany next door.

"They ought to billet the Germans here," laughed Gunnar.

Irene hit out at him. Gunnar lifted her off the floor. Meanwhile Lars was looking at a black delivery bike lying flat on the grass. Its seat was much too small for it, and it bore the words *Kolstrup Brickyard.*

Irene came over to him. "Are you in a dreamworld?"

Lars quickly glanced away, not wanting to look her straight in the eye. She had a very penetrating way of looking at you. More than once, she had let that glance of hers dwell on a point on his cheek and then travel on, down over his nose to his mouth, to his lips. He felt almost—almost as if she were kissing him with her eyes.

"This bike must have been mended a million times," remarked Gunnar.

"Do *you* think this is a pit?" she asked.

Lars walked across the room. "No, I don't. In fact, I like it here. Ruins have their own beauty."

"And the moral of that is . . . ?" asked Gunnar, looking at Irene.

Irene glanced briefly at Lars, but then went over and rammed her knee into Gunnar's hip so that he fell flat on the floor. When Lars looked out the window again, the delivery bike was gone. That both worried and intrigued him. Someone else had been here with them. Maybe even in the old café itself. Someone from the brickyard, which actually was a long way away.

Rosen and Father were talking heatedly about the war, the Allies' chances, the death of the Danish Social Democrat leader Stauning, the new hymnals for church. Gunnar was involved in the conversation too. Lars looked at his mother; she was darning socks. Irene was leafing through a fashion magazine from 1936.

"There were a lot of German soldiers in church this evening," Mother remarked.

Father muttered something to the effect that one could hardly tell them to stay away.

"Well, no, they're better churchgoers than most Danes," Mother continued, putting the lid on her sewing basket.

"I'd have thought their God lived in the führer's bunker in Berlin," said Rosen.

Father laughed and shook his head. "Ah, well," he said, "I suppose at heart they're human beings of a sort, my dear Rosen, despite their uniforms."

Gunnar got to his feet.

"Nevertheless, I'd like to see them out of here," he said forcefully. "The whole bunch of them."

Father sighed and made a small movement with his right

hand. It meant: All right, Gunnar, take it easy. We're not so badly off. There are many in a worse way.

Soon after that, Irene said good night. Gunnar would walk her home. Lars saw them standing in the hall. Gunnar kissed her gently and whispered something in her ear. Lars couldn't help watching. Nor could he help wondering what Gunnar found to say to her.

Do you wear corsets, madam?

Do you want to come over to the church and sit in the back pew with me? There's something I'd like to show you.

Do I get a kiss this evening, Irene? A long, slow kiss?

A little later they left. The house was quiet. Rosen was sitting there, perhaps meditating on some quotation from Confucius while gazing gloomily at his Danish cigar, which had nothing but smoke to offer—and he'd been to South America and smoked real Havana cigars! Cigars rolled on the brown thighs of South American girls. Oh, Lord!

In the study, the grandfather clock ticked away, slicing the evening into small identical bits. A dog barked in the distance. It was nearly ten o'clock. Now they would sit and doze, chat, and philosophize for another quarter of an hour, and then his mother would say, "Well, my dears, time for bed if we're to be up with the chickens."

America! Or maybe Canada. Texas, Kansas, Oklahoma, Arizona. Across the hills and far away, over the red steppes, surrounded by a sweet fragrance of exotic cigars rolled on the thighs of young girls.

He went into the kitchen and heard his mother blow the candles out.

Lars said good night. His mother's eyes twinkled at him. His father seemed to be fast asleep in his wing chair. Rosen's face had disappeared behind clouds of grayish blue smoke.

It would soon be summer vacation. And this summer he would be doing something different! Lars knew Gunnar had plans, plenty of them, and Luffe too.

Lars stood on the porch. There were no trees overhead. He had the evidence of his new status in his pocket: the key to the loft. The right to go up there anytime he liked.

He heard his mother rinse the cups in the sink, while his father, awake again, preached one of his little sermons to Rosen, whose own mind had long ago flown to Cuba.

"You see, Rosen, it's not that we want to get rid of you, heaven forbid, but what with the way the war's going, and from all we hear . . ."

"Good night, Mrs. Balstrup!" called Rosen. That was the way he brushed aside any allusion to his Jewish origins.

Lars went upstairs. A little later he was closing the loft door behind him. He toured the place like a conqueror. Then he went down to the belfry. From its two narrow windows he could see most of the parish. The fresh smell of summer was in the air. He felt it calling him. The water of the fjord was shining; it would not let the daylight go. Farther off were rolling fields where yellow mustard glowed in the dusk. Such peace and calm. Not a sign of war. Here and there you could even see people out tending their vegetable plots.

Over to the left lay the airfield. It was being extended to give the Germans a base for an airlift to Oslo. Work on the extension provided jobs for many of the unemployed. Farther to the right were the chimneys of the brewery, and beyond them the shanty settlement where the brickyard workers lived.

Lars smiled to himself.

"I know something about you, dirt face, whoever you are," he whispered.

That was one of the things he had not told Gunnar. For a few days after they cycled out to the old café, Lars had waited outside the Kolstrup Brickyard around quitting time. He had had no luck the first day, but the day after that he had recognized the clumsy black delivery bike with its small seat. The boy riding it wasn't much older than he himself was; younger, if anything. It had been hard to tell, because his face was so grimy. Lars followed him to see whether he did indeed live in the shanty settlement. But what was someone like that doing in the café in the woods, miles from home? Three days later Lars got his answer. His patience paid off.

The boy cycled out to the café again after work—with Lars a suitable distance behind him. They made good time. When he finally reached the café, the boy checked to see that no one was inside before disappearing up the back stairs. Lars waited ten minutes. Then the boy came out and pedaled away. Lars waited another fifteen minutes before he headed up the back stairs.

He found himself in a place where pigeons roosted, a cross between a loft and a lumber room. Ten minutes later he discovered a metal box, which he took over to the light. It contained a pack of English cigarettes, a pair of horn-rimmed glasses, a necklace that looked quite valuable, a swastika badge, and a German pistol wrapped in a dirty cloth. Lars gasped.

A real Luger.

He put everything back in the box. It would be stupid to ride around with a German Luger in the evening, when the risk of being stopped and searched was ten times greater than during the day.

Better to wait a few days.

An hour later he had cycled home, carrying a secret in the back of his mind and a picture of the boy with the dirty face engraved on his retina.

At last the light was gone. Night fell. A truck full of German soldiers rattled over the bridge toward the center of town.

"Just wait," murmured Lars. "Just you wait."

THREE

Crew training on the fjord had intensified now that there were only six weeks to go until the big regatta. There was no need for Lars to urge the eight oarsmen on; all he had to do was follow the rhythm of the boat with his upper body and steer it. The sound of the oars on the water, of the sliding seats on their runners, soon merged with the crew's heavy breathing.

Within a month they had to get the whole thing operating like a metronome, Lars thought. Out here on the water nothing else mattered. School and exams were left behind. Stroke after stroke, day after day, nothing but sea and sky.

Their training was followed with great interest. Former oarsmen from the students' club shouted encouragement and offered advice. The regatta was something everyone could rally around, a fine old tradition that had nothing, nothing whatsoever to do with the Germans.

Then one day, when Lars and Gunnar were the first ones to arrive at the handsome boathouse, where sculls, canoes, and shells lay side by side on long racks, Gunnar suddenly turned on his heel and stared at a tall thin man wearing a raincoat. A raincoat was all wrong for this time of year.

Lars knew he had seen the man before, in the library. Lars had accidentally dropped a church bookmark, and the man had picked it up and given it back to him with a small aloof smile. It was a curious gesture. He had held the bookmark just a little too long—long enough for it to seem odd. The man was blond and reminded Lars of a tropical fish Luffe once had. A sucker fish. Luffe said it cleaned algae off the aquarium glass. The man wore the small round Nazi badge stuck in his lapel. It was as if he wanted to let Lars know the gestapo had been in town, just for the record. And now here he was again, in the boathouse, walking around calmly, almost as if he were bored, running his hand along the elegant sloping sides of the boats.

"Beautiful," he said. "Splendid."

For some reason Lars had expected the man to speak German, or anyway to have a German accent. But he sounded as Danish as they come.

He wished them a good wind, which was silly, since they rowed best in the calm. Maybe it was a joke. If so, it didn't strike either brother as funny.

Lars and Gunnar sat close together in the boat. Now and then Lars caught Gunnar looking straight at him in a new way, with a different kind of concentration. Or maybe it was just his imagination. Maybe, thought Lars, gazing out over the fjord, maybe it's just my guilty conscience. Should I feel guilty?

On the wall above Rosen's little desk were lots of watercolor paintings. They had all been sent to him from Hildesheim, a small town in Germany. You could make out neat blue handwriting on the backs of the pictures. On the front each said *Filip and Nina*. That was all; always the same words. The paintings themselves were ordinary little landscapes: sunlit scenes of northern Germany. Above all, there was no sign of war in them. Lars did not know very much about this Nina, except that Rosen had met her in the early 1930s in Lund, Sweden, when he was a guest organist at Lund Cathedral. They had been corresponding regularly ever since. Nina had never come to Denmark to visit Rosen, but Rosen had gone to Germany twice. Lars's mother said he went wherever the tide took him.

"Are you lovers?" Lars had asked Rosen last Christmas, regretting his question the moment it was out. Rosen never locked his door. He counted on people not to barge in without knocking. On that occasion, Lars *had* barged in—he could tell from the look on the little organist's face. Rosen's fine features wore a resigned, faraway expression. Three days later he commented, "It's not easy, loving by mail."

It was a passing remark made in the vestry, a slightly dry

comment, and when Rosen left, Lars had added, "Yes, and in secret too."

Why was he thinking of Filip Rosen just now? No doubt because one of Fräulein Nina's pictures showed a river scene, probably the banks of the Weser River, in Germany.

They rowed out to the turning point marked by the yellow buoy, where Gunnar gave himself and his crew a well-earned rest.

Søren was not happy about the three false strokes he had made on the way out. One of the others complained that there was too much pull on the starboard side, upsetting their rhythm.

"Lars will have to correct that," murmured Gunnar, letting his gaze travel along the banks, from the roofs in town out to the Kolstrup Brickyard.

He glanced briefly at Lars, who had been following his gaze. They said nothing to each other, but Lars felt that Gunnar knew something. Knew more than he was going to say right then.

The meeting of the group began in the usual way. They had a list of things to discuss, an agenda; Søren was in charge. Lars sat at the end of the table with Luffe, who was always fiddling with something; today it was a model locomotive. For some reason or other Lars felt slightly disappointed. This was his first real meeting, so perhaps he'd expected too much. He'd hoped for something more exciting than just planning to steal the license plate from a German truck in Østergade and puncture its tires.

The meeting began with everyone singing the Norwegian national anthem, in honor of the groups they had modeled themselves on. Lars had no objection to singing: It took him by surprise, that was all. Søren and Gunnar stood at attention. After singing, when they reached "other business" in their agenda, Luffe said he wanted to bring up something they'd discussed at a previous meeting; would that be in order? Gunnar said yes. Then Luffe said he just thought he'd mention that he'd made a key to fit the main building at the airfield. He broke into his usual silly giggle.

Lars smiled at him. Luffe was in high spirits. Lars knew that Luffe's father worked on the railroad, and his mother was a cleaning lady. It was something of a mystery to both parents that they'd produced such a talented son. They lived in a white cottage with a garden that they tended meticulously. Most of it was vegetables, but in addition, Luffe's father had built a greenhouse the size of an aircraft hangar. Lars's mother always said Luffe's mother could work wonders with practically no money at all.

Luffe had a workshop down in the basement where he had been doing experiments since the age of seven. Gunnar and Luffe were already friends in elementary school. Søren came later. Luffe was still in elementary school when he invented his automatic parachute, which they tested on Søren's hamster Thorvald by throwing the little creature out of the belfry. Søren got another hamster later, and they stuck to their decision not to try any more of Luffe's experiments for five years. By then Luffe knew so much physics and chemistry that he thought the time was right to go public. The event took place in the meadow outside the brewery. Several of the brewery workers stopped on their way home to watch the first flight of Oluf the Cannon King.

Luffe had welded the pipes together himself. They made a funnel eighteen feet long, tilted at a forty-five degree angle, which was the launching pad. Gunnar said Luffe had worn a red Cannon King cape and a painted crash helmet. A boy called Max was supposed to light the fuse. Luffe had calculated that he would fly exactly forty-six feet into the air—measured from the pipe, that is—and would then make a gentle arc and land in some bales of straw a little way off.

There were about forty in the audience for this experiment, the result of which was that Max lost his hearing for two months and Luffe endured second-degree burns on his feet. People said Luffe got off lightly. Luffe said the experiment only whetted his appetite for more.

Several of his later experiments did work. They even worked well.

And now it seemed he'd copied a German key.

Søren looked at Gunnar and shook his head in irritation. "Oh, really! I thought we'd exhausted that subject," he snapped.

Luffe took the big key out of his pocket.

"It's OK," said Gunnar. "We can talk about it, now that the posters are ready."

Lars looked from one to the other of them. "What posters?"

Luffe carried them over from the corner where they had

been lying rolled up. In red and black lettering they bore slogans meant to remind the Danes of the day of the German invasion, and of their freedom, things like *Remember April 9th* and *Denmark Free Again.*

Søren explained that the posters were to be put up all over town, especially in busy places, to show people that not everyone had given up, that there were still some who were prepared to fight for Denmark.

"Fight for Denmark?" exclaimed Lars. "With posters?"

They ignored him. Luffe said he knew the schedule of guard shifts at the airfield.

Søren looked at him with a little smile. "Oh, yes, and have the dogs been informed about it? The whole place is swarming with Rottweilers and Dobermans, you know."

Luffe merely shrugged. Arguing was not his style.

"Leaving that aside," added Søren, with a glance toward Gunnar, "we ought to take a vote on the airfield-building idea."

Lars put his hand up.

"Our new member has the floor," said Søren.

"Look, I'm sorry," began Lars, "but what exactly are we doing? I thought—well, I thought we were serious. I mean —street signs and license plates, caps and flat tires. That sort of stuff's not going to stop Hitler!"

"It makes the Germans look silly," said Søren. "Totally ridiculous."

"About the airfield building . . . ," Luffe tried again.

Søren shook his head in a resigned way. "Luffe, we *have* discussed the airfield building. The place is guarded by dogs, right? What will little Luffe do when one of those monsters comes bounding up with its tongue hanging out? Say 'Here, doggie'?"

Lars looked down at the table. "We could shoot it," he said.

There was silence in the loft.

"Shoot it," repeated Luffe, hopefully. "What with?"

Lars looked up. "Our new Luger."

He had their full attention now.

"Oh, really? We have a Luger?" Gunnar sounded hesitant.

Lars said he knew where they could easily find one. He explained how he had stumbled on it by accident, out at the old café. But he made no mention of the boy from the brickyard.

As chairman, Søren replied first. "Where do you think a gun like that comes from? From the Germans, of course. Stolen property. Is that what we want? Gunnar! Is that why we founded the St. Petri Group? Anyway, Lars, what you say sounds simple enough, but which one of us can handle a gun like that? Which of us could shoot someone or something down in cold blood? Could you, Lars? Well, come on, could you? How about you, Luffe? You can't even step on a piddling little ant! Anyway, how do you think the Germans are going to react if we suddenly start firing guns on the airfield?"

Søren's voice had grown calm. He even gave Lars a friendly smile. Gunnar nodded. Lars knew that those two almost never disagreed. They were friends in the true sense of the word. The only thing they didn't share was Irene. When Gunnar went to Copenhagen to study theology, Søren planned to go as well, to study law. They intended to make their way through life side by side, supporting and helping each other. They'd be lifelong friends.

Gunnar took out his pipe. Lars knew what that meant. Gunnar needed time to think. He wasn't automatically on Søren's side; Luffe knew that too. With a dreamy look in his eyes, he asked Lars about the Luger. Lars said it was in a metal box, and of course Søren was right, someone must have stolen it. But why not take it when it was there anyway? For safety's sake.

With a forceful movement, Søren leaned over the table.

"That's just where you're wrong, Lars," he said. "For safety's sake we ought to leave it there. Can't you all see that? Once we start messing with that sort of thing, it'll get out of control. One day for no good reason we'll start thinking, Well, since we have it, we might as well use it, and then there'll be the devil to pay."

Gunnar turned back to the table, puffing on his pipe. His shadow fell across the nearest arch.

"I agree with Søren," he said. "But we can't just leave it there. Of course we're not going to shoot any dogs out on the airfield, but a time might come when we could use it. I suggest we go get it tomorrow after practice. It might as well be here as in the old café."

The next day they bicycled out through the pale green beech wood. Lars rode beside Søren, who asked him about Kirsten. She was friends with Søren's younger sister. Her family and

Søren's had become very close over the last ten years or so. The attorney and the doctor: Søren's father and Kirsten's father.

"We're almost like one big family." Søren smiled, aiming a playful punch at Lars, who just shook his head, thinking of pretty, elegant Kirsten when she waved to him in the school yard, walking arm in arm with Søren's sister. She really was very pretty. And very sweet, very fond of him. She was good-natured too, always cheerful. And athletic; good at tennis. She'd make someone a fine wife, the doctor's pretty Kirsten.

I don't know why I keep her at a distance, talking nonsense to her, Lars thought to himself. And a small voice answered: You know perfectly well why, you miserable liar.

Ahead of them, Gunnar and Luffe were racing downhill, bumping into each other. Lars liked to see Gunnar with Luffe. Then he was the old Gunnar again, the Gunnar Lars remembered from their childhood.

They came out onto the public path, where Gunnar and Luffe passed two German soldiers sitting on a bench, smoking. One of the soldiers even said a friendly "Good afternoon."

As Gunnar observed later, "The worst thing is when they're friendly, especially the old soldiers. They expect you to be friendly back. It's the horrible way they take it for granted. As if they were saying: Come on, relax—well, yes, so we did occupy your little country and take over your best houses and move into them, and yes, we do go out with some of your girls now and then, and we expect you to stand aside when we walk down the street, but so what? Is that so bad? After all, in your hearts there are quite a few of you who think Hitler has the right idea. Isn't that so? The Danes hate disorder too. "

The café was right where it had always been, as if it were simply waiting for better times to come.

It was evening now. The big trees made the twilight gloomy. A cuckoo called above the treetops, its cries blending in with the hoots of the little ferry out on the fjord. So many things haven't changed at all, thought Lars, and yet it's impossible to breathe. He went over to the dilapidated kitchen door, which was partly open.

Talking to one another, they went up the steep stairs and came out in the dark oblong of the loft, where the pigeons lived. Last time Lars had been there, the birds had startled him as they suddenly fluttered up through the hole in the roof. The place was quiet now. He switched his flashlight on and started looking for the metal box.

"It ought to be here. . . ."

Where were those pigeons, anyway? What had happened to them?

Luffe giggled for no apparent reason. Søren sat down a little way off and crossed his arms. Gunnar helped Lars search.

"Sure it wasn't just a nail file you saw?" Søren grinned.

"It has to be here, unless somehow somebody moved it," muttered Lars. And then he glanced at Gunnar, who was not searching anymore but simply staring into the dim light behind Søren. Lars felt fear constrict him. His earlier uneasiness grew overwhelming.

A dirty, smudged face appeared behind Søren. A dirty face with bright, furious eyes. An animal . . . a desperate animal. But animals don't carry guns, and now Lars knew why they hadn't found the box containing the Luger, because its muzzle was pointing straight at Søren's temple. Everyone stiffened, not least the terrified Søren, who sat there rigid.

"Gunnar," he gasped, "can't you . . . ?"

Lars was just putting out an arm in a gesture of appeasement when the boy behind Søren hissed at them.

"Get out!" he said. "Get out, all of you."

Luffe was first down the stairs. But Gunnar clearly didn't want to leave Søren sitting there alone.

Lars nodded to Gunnar and glanced back at the boy from the brickyard again. He was desperate and frightened. A nasty situation.

Gunnar went slowly down to join Luffe, who was claiming the gun wasn't loaded. Gunnar shushed him.

Up in the loft, Lars tried to reassure the boy through his look and his gestures.

"Come down, Lars," called Gunnar.

As Lars started to go over to the stairs, the boy nearly kicked Søren down to join the others.

"We weren't going to steal anything," muttered Lars darkly as he followed Søren down. Soon after that, all was quiet.

They raced out of the café, Gunnar trying to calm Søren, who was so angry he was almost foaming at the mouth.

"It'll be a long time," he said furiously, "a very long time before we listen to Lars Balstrup again."

Lars got on his bike, while Søren pointed a threatening

finger at the upper story of the café. "And as for you, you little turd," he shouted, "we'll get you yet, you can bet on it!"

Three sharp reports rang out over the woods, echoing in the distance. Two tiles clattered down from the roof.

Gunnar, Søren, Luffe, and Lars pedaled off madly into the night.

F O U R

Lars was going home from school with Gunnar. It was the last day of the semester, and everyone was feeling cheerful. Despite the Germans, summer had arrived, as the principal said before they all dispersed.

Gunnar was in high spirits and seemed to have forgotten all about the episode in the old café. He dragged Lars off to Algade, where he stopped in front of a store: Olsson Jewelers and Goldsmiths.

A sudden thought shot through Lars's head: Robbery! Saint Gunnar's going to cut his angel wings off and break into Olsson's jewelry store. But Gunnar's beaming face quickly put that idea to rest.

They went over to the window.

Gunnar pointed, and Lars saw them at once, lying side by side on a piece of black velvet like the store's showpiece.

"Real silver," said Gunnar reverently.

Lars said nothing. The rings were pretty, very simple—very obviously symbolizing fidelity.

Gunnar slapped him lightly on the back. "You're the only one who knows," he said. "I was thinking of announcing it at the regatta. That would be a good time, don't you think?"

"Yes, sure," muttered Lars, imagining Irene. Irene walking across the school yard in her floral-print summer dress with the white collar, in her ankle socks and soft braided leather shoes. Like Princess Tove of Denmark. Fresh as dew, lovely as amber.

Gunnar was talking away, about the café incident now. Lars wasn't to worry, he said, it hadn't been his fault. There was nothing wrong with the actual idea. Søren's ruffled feathers had been smoothed.

They went into the coffee shop, which was very full. Gunnar went over to buy cookies and hot chocolate. Lars, watching him standing at the counter, felt something deep inside him open up like a trapdoor.

Gunnar put the tray down on the table. His cheeks were flushed; he was full of plans.

"Do you think I ought to tell them first? Mother and Father, I mean."

Lars looked at him and thought: I'm looking straight into heaven. He cleared his throat, feeling an uncomfortable sweaty sensation.

"Gunnar," he mumbled, "there's something—something I ought to tell you."

He stopped, twisting his hands together under the table. Gunnar took a bite out of his cookie.

"It's about—well, it's about . . ."

"So, spit it out. What's on your mind?"

Lars glanced at the corner, where three German soldiers were telling four Danes to move aside for them.

"It's about the Kolstrup Brickyard."

"What about the Kolstrup Brickyard?"

"That's where the Luger came from," Lars said flatly. "I've been . . . kind of keeping an eye on the boy who stole it. He's no older than me. Well, you saw him yourself. He lives in the shanty settlement. Of course I didn't know he was there at the old café, but—I was thinking, suppose I got to know him? He could be a useful man to have in reserve."

"As a kind of orderly, you mean? Carrying messages?"

"Yes, something like that."

Gunnar thought the suggestion over and shook his head. "It's too dangerous to let in someone like that," he said.

"But suppose we could get hold of the pistol?"

Gunnar drained his cup.

"I'm not going to discuss that. But listen . . . if you do get to know him, promise me not to give anything away. You've taken an oath, remember."

"What is there to give away?" snapped Lars. "You and Søren and Luffe have stolen a few license plates, right?"

Gunnar broke into a big forgiving smile and loosened his tie.

"OK, little brother," he said. "Now then, tell me honestly, what do you think of those rings?"

The Kolstrup Brickyard lay outside town. Together with the brewery, it was one of the two main local employers. Both firms were now under German control, so their production lines had been reorganized.

Lars had already hung around the brickyard several times, waiting for the shift to let out. This time he went in through the gates, ignoring the German guard who glanced at him without much interest. Exactly ten minutes later the whistle sounded for quitting time. The brickyard workers came pouring out, dirty and tired. Lars soon spotted the boy. He was by himself, and empty-handed, which seemed rather odd, since all the other workers had lunch pails.

"Hey, you—just a moment!"

The boy turned slowly and looked at Lars without any particular surprise.

Lars gestured. "Can we talk for a couple of minutes?"

"What about?" The boy's voice was hoarse, wary, maybe a little reproachful. His face wore a brooding expression, with the hint of an unhappy frown. Perhaps he was just tired.

Lars scuffed the ground with his foot, and the two engagement rings on black velvet flashed before him.

"Look, I'm sorry about what happened the other day. It was my fault in a way. I mean, if I'd known it was yours . . ."

They went around to the back of the factory complex, where

44

a rather scruffy stretch of grass led down to the fjord. Lars walked beside the boy, who didn't look at him but just pushed his clumsy old bike.

"I—my name's Lars," said Lars, more to keep the conversation going than anything else. "Lars Balstrup. My father's the minister here."

This did not appear to make much of an impression. The boy picked at the fabric cover of his bicycle seat with a dirty finger.

"Like I said," persisted Lars, "of course we won't tell anyone anything about . . . about . . ."

"It's not there anymore. I moved it."

Lars looked at the boy's hands. They were big and coarse. Most of all they were filthy.

"Listen," said Lars. "I don't know if you can keep a secret."

The boy looked as if the word *secret* had been spoken in a foreign language.

"You see—" Lars stopped, smiling slightly at himself and this hopeless situation. There was something about this boy, something he'd noticed the first time he set eyes on him. A defiance. A . . . a dogged determination, along with a disarming vulnerability.

"Can I ask you your name?"

"Me? My name's Otto."

Lars nodded, as if that made all the difference. Then the boy added, "Hvidemann."

He said his surname in a different tone, with a touch of pride. Lars took this as an opening.

"Otto," he said point-blank, "we're working on something—me and the others, I mean. Working against the Germans. I'm telling you this in confidence, obviously."

The boy didn't look at him, but he seemed to be taking in every word.

"And we could certainly use that Luger."

When Otto said nothing, Lars continued, on his own account and not Gunnar's this time. "And we were saying—in the group, that is—that we could use a sort of orderly too."

They looked at each other. The word *orderly* hung in the air between them like something foreign, slowly comprehended. Then Otto said, "I can get hold of most things."

He spoke in a slightly gloomy, matter-of-fact tone, as if seeing to such matters was his melancholy fate. Lars looked searchingly at him.

"Great, Otto. That's great. It's just that the pistol—how can I put it?—comes into the picture. Do you know what I mean?"

Otto nodded and looked at his dirty hands.

"I could bring it along if you like."

Lars strode beside him in a businesslike way.

"Well, yes, you could, but maybe it would be better if I took it?"

"I'd rather deliver it myself."

Lars sighed, not at all surprised.

"Suppose we say you bring it along this evening?" he said. "To St. Petri."

"The church?"

"The church, yes. Go around back, to the left of the main door. To the old door that the women used to enter through."

Lars smiled, with no idea why. Otto wasn't smiling, anyway.

"How about eight o'clock?"

"Nine."

Otto took the handlebars of his bike and wheeled it calmly off toward the brickyard. Clearly he had things to do, but he moved quietly and calmly, like a person whose life had fallen into a set routine very early, and who didn't spend much time wondering why.

Lars, on the other hand, hurried as he cycled back to town and up the hill to where the church stood, thinking that there was likely to be a lot of trouble with Søren and Gunnar. Nevertheless, so far as Lars could see, this Otto Hvidemann was worth it.

F I V E

Irene had come to dinner. As usual, she fit easily into the family—as sister-in-law, daughter-in-law, and girlfriend. Conversation over the steaming fish fillets was sporadic; Gunnar and his mother kept it going. Now and then the minister murmured something or other unintelligible, as if to show that he wasn't asleep.

Lars suspected him of using his robes, the church, and even religion as a kind of camouflage for a completely different world, a totally different existence. His attitude toward the war was clear and straightforward: He went about his business and lived his daily life as usual, but he seldom missed a chance to show where he stood. His position emerged in casual remarks he let drop in his sermons, in his choice of hymns, and in his reaction when anyone overstepped his limits—for in spite of the minister's amiable manner, his limits were clear. He followed "the course of the combat," as he called it, with an interest that he otherwise devoted only to his stamp collection. He listened avidly to the radio —the broadcasts from London were positively sacred—and entered bulletins from the fronts on his personal ordnance survey map with accuracy and precision. He might say to Rosen, "Rommel will be hard to beat. On the other hand, the Germans are doing badly in Russia. But they're only one hundred twenty miles from Alexandria now, and I don't like that."

Rosen himself seldom discussed the war. He ate in silence, listening politely to everyone else, speaking only when someone asked him a question. Perhaps his even-temperedness called for greater sacrifice than anyone imagined.

Irene sat at the end of the table, next to Gunnar. Tonight she was quieter than usual. Her presence often had a cheering effect on them all, even causing Reverend Balstrup to remember old jokes, although seldom their punch lines. Gunnar was regaling everyone with tales of Junkersen, a teacher at school who had given his class an hour-long lecture about the Aryan race. Junkersen was very pro-German and began by listing those Indo-European characteristics that he described as noble, distinguished, and elevated—in short, non-Jewish.

"What a nerve the man has!" said Gunnar angrily, his cheeks flushed, as he speared a potato. But Lars thought his brother was as sunny as ever, really, his cheerful good temper showing through his anger like a bright coin in calm water.

Reverend Balstrup murmured something about the word *Aryan* originally coming from the Sanskrit. Then Rosen observed quietly that Junkersen wasn't the only one: It was a fact that many other Danes found it difficult to get along with Jews.

There was silence around the table.

"I don't mean to spoil your appetite," added Rosen. "Come to think of it, there are plenty of Jews I don't get along with myself."

Gunnar and his father laughed. Good humor was restored; they all drank to one another in buttermilk. Then, suddenly, Mrs. Balstrup was in the middle of a lively story about Mr. Samson, who used to live by the railroad tracks. Over the years, his little basement shop grew to be the town's leading clothing store, going from a stock of buttons and ribbons to fine fabrics, rugs, leather, and furs. Finally Mr. Samson bought the whole building and the house next door as well. By the time he moved away to Sweden, he was employing eighteen people.

"And the ugly little fellow sat there at his cash register all day long counting his money. That was the only idea he had in his head—money, money, and more money. . . ."

Mrs. Balstrup, who had been warming to her subject, suddenly stopped. Again there was silence around the table. Gunnar fidgeted self-consciously with his napkin ring while Reverend Balstrup concentrated on an inoffensive fish bone.

With a start, Mrs. Balstrup looked at Filip Rosen, who smiled and laid his hand over hers.

Lars felt a lump rise in his throat. He knew it was not only because of Rosen the organist; it was because the day had been so—well, confusing. There'd been the meeting with Otto Hvidemann, but most of all, there had been the two silver rings on the piece of black velvet. And now Rosen.

"I tell you what," said the organist, patting Mrs. Balstrup's hand. "I've been keeping a bottle of old port by me. It came from Prague. I thought we might try it after dinner."

"To be sure, strong drink is the devil's own work," murmured Reverend Balstrup, "so bring out your bottle, Rosen, and let's get it over with!"

Irene and Mrs. Balstrup cleared the table. Lars looked at Irene's hands as she picked up the dishes. Especially at her ring finger. She was wearing a cream-colored ivory band on it. A young girl's ring, a ring she'd probably bought for herself. It suited her brown, suntanned hand. It was a mark of freedom, unlike the silver fetter on black velvet. His mother tied her apron on. Now she would rinse the dishes, wash them, and make coffee, in that order.

"I wish I could take you to the South Seas with me," Lars whispered to himself.

"The hell with Junkersen!"

Lars turned around. Gunnar was talking to himself as he filled his pipe. He beckoned Lars out into the hallway.

"Did you talk to that boy?"

Lars nodded. "His name's Otto."

Gunnar shook his head, smiling.

"What's so funny about that?"

"Nothing. Tell me what's bothering you, little brother."
Gunnar made Lars turn around so that they were facing each
other.

"Nothing's bothering me."

"You didn't tell him anything, did you? About us?"

"Of course I didn't. But I think he's willing to let us have
the gun."

Gunnar drew on his pipe and looked approvingly at Lars.
Irene came out to join them.

"So this is where you two are hiding!"

Gunnar blew smoke in her face and put an arm around
her.

"What are you talking about that's so secret?" She looked
at Lars.

"Junkersen," replied Gunnar.

"Women," said Lars.

Gunnar burst out laughing. "Listen to the expert!"

Lars started to leave.

"Are you still going out with that pretty girl Kirsten?" Irene
called after him.

He opened the hall door.

"Oh, just one isn't enough for me," he said dryly, and
closed the door.

He could hear them go into the living room. He stood there
for a moment, leaning against the door frame. Why am I such
an idiot? he thought. Why do I always have to shoot my mouth
off? And why do I have to turn brick red just because she
asks me to pass the gravy boat?

One hour later he was at the church, watching Otto wheel

his black delivery bike up the hill. Only now did Lars realize what he had asked the other boy to do: cycle right through town with a stolen Luger under his shirt. People were sometimes stopped and searched in town. Not often, but sometimes.

"Thanks for coming." He took Otto into the church.

Otto looked around hesitantly. He had just washed, and he smelled of coarse household soap.

"Did you bring it?" Lars was fidgeting slightly.

Otto tapped his chest.

"Listen, the others are up there—they're still not too pleased about what happened out at the old café, so . . . well, I thought, suppose you gave me the gun now?"

Otto looked at him. Blankly.

"The thing is," pursued Lars, "I can't—can't actually let you in. Not right away. You do understand, don't you?"

Otto looked at his feet. He was wearing clogs. "Yes," he said quietly, "but if I'm going to be an orderly . . . ?"

Lars cleared his throat. "Look, I know what. Wait here a couple of minutes, Otto, just a couple of minutes."

He raced up all the thousand stairs and was out of breath when he arrived in the loft. Søren was talking about fat Göring and a cartoon he'd seen. Luffe came straight over to Lars.

"Did you get it?"

Lars looked at Gunnar, who was sitting with his feet up on the table. They were all drinking tea.

"No. Well, yes and no . . . I mean, the Luger's down there, but—er, well, he—he's—I mean, the boy from out at the café—he's here too."

Luffe broke into a wide grin. "The pistol's Big Daddy."

Gunnar stood up. "You mean the boy from the brickyard is here, in the church?"

Lars gestured helplessly.

Søren shook his head.

"Have you brought that boy up here?" whispered Gunnar reproachfully.

"I told you, didn't I? He's down by the door. I thought we were interested in getting the gun."

Luffe agreed that they were. But Søren was skeptical. A dumb working kid—a thief . . .

"OK," shouted Lars, feeling he had had about enough. "OK, but maybe he can get ahold of more than thumbtacks and cardboard for us! I thought we were in this for real. Pardon me if there's something I failed to grasp. . . ."

"Take it easy, OK?" said Gunnar. "We'd like to have that pistol. Of course we want it. But surely it's clear that we can't afford any risks. Obviously he can't just come up here. You can tell him this—you can tell Otto we'll meet him tomorrow down at the meadow by the fjord."

Lars put his hands on his hips. "Gunnar, we can't do that. Not now that he's come all the way here. We can't simply tell him to go away again."

"Forget it, Lars," said Søren. "We can't let just anyone from the brickyard come barging in."

"I'm not talking about just anyone."

"Why don't we go down and talk to this kid now?" suggested Luffe.

They looked at him. Gunnar shrugged his shoulders. "OK," he said. "Tell him we'll meet inside the church."

"Inside the church," repeated Lars.

"Yes, inside the church."

Otto Hvidemann had never been in St. Petri before. It was one of the country's largest and oldest churches, and it looked particularly gloomy in the evening when no lights were on and shadows fell through the tall windows.

Otto and Lars walked slowly toward the altar.

"The church was built between 1682 and 1696," whispered Lars helpfully.

Otto stared at the huge vaults, each supported by four powerful columns. Angels and demons stared down from the ceiling.

They sat down in the front row of pews. Ten minutes later the door behind them opened. They turned around and saw Gunnar silhouetted in the doorway, with Søren on one side and Luffe on the other.

Otto stared in bewilderment as they marched slowly forward, looking like a firing squad.

Gunnar stationed himself at the side of the pew as he said, "Lars says you have something for us."

Otto stood up and put his hand inside his shirt. He brought out the pistol.

Gunnar looked at it appraisingly. Luffe forgot his role and giggled delightedly.

"I can get more ammunition too," said Otto.

Gunnar nodded, took the gun, and handed it to Søren, who, without looking at it, slipped it into his pocket.

"What else are you called, besides Otto?" Gunnar's deep voice sounded stern and imposing in the big church.

"Hvidemann," said Otto quietly. "Otto Hvidemann."

"Where do you live?"

Lars looked at Gunnar, puzzled. "Is this some kind of interrogation, Gunnar?"

Gunnar ignored him and repeated his question.

Otto said he lived out behind the brickyard, at Number 18.

"You mean in the shanty settlement?"

Otto nodded.

"And you work at the Kolstrup Brickyard. Do you have any brothers and sisters?"

"Yes, two sisters," said Otto, "but they're only little."

"What does your father do?"

Otto looked down. "My father's dead," he whispered.

Lars glared at Gunnar, who was momentarily struck dumb. Luffe had stopped giggling.

"What does your mother do?" asked Gunnar.

Otto said she was a waitress.

"We need to know about you," Gunnar went on. "So far, we know where you live, your name, and your job—and we know you've stolen a German pistol. But what really matters, Otto Hvidemann, is that you don't know *us*. You've never been here in your life and you'll never show you recognize us. Right?"

Lars glanced at Otto, who looked as if he didn't understand a word of this.

"You must never, I repeat *never*, contact us," Gunnar continued. "If we need you, we'll find you. Our plans require that we take these precautions."

Gunnar nodded to Søren and Luffe. The next moment they were walking back to the church door.

Lars looked at Otto, who was still standing by the pew, his hand crumpling the loose part of his shirt. Then his voice rang out right through the church, reaching Gunnar, Luffe, and Søren just as they got to the door.

"Give me my pistol back!"

Gunnar stopped as if changed to stone. He turned, an incredulous expression on his face. "What did you say?"

Slowly, he walked back. Lars stood up. Gunnar's attitude was downright menacing now.

"Can we talk for a moment, Gunnar?" asked Lars.

Søren said he was sick of all this kindergarten stuff.

"Give me my pistol back," Otto repeated without looking at any of them.

"But you've just given it to us," Luffe pointed out, utterly logical.

Otto glanced up. "Yes, well, but I thought—I thought I was going to—going to be one of your group," he said quietly.

Søren wrinkled his brow and sat down in a pew, checking his watch with pointed irritation.

"We—we can't discuss that," said Gunnar.

"Why in the world not?" asked Lars.

Søren stood up. "Oh, come on, Gunnar, let's give him his crappy little gun back. I've had enough of this nonsense."

Gunnar hesitated and looked at Luffe, who shrugged. His glance moved on to Lars, who was standing behind Otto.

"He knows who we are already," murmured Luffe.

"So he does. Very funny, right?" said Søren.

Gunnar led Søren over to a corner. Three minutes passed while they conducted a heated argument, their voices low.

Lars glanced at Luffe, who smiled broadly and held his fingers up in the shape of a gun. Then Gunnar came back, looking very official.

"Otto Hvidemann," he said, speaking with studied calm. "Do you see that big chandelier up there, hanging from the ceiling?"

S I X

Work on the local airfield had not been under way for very long, but now the effort to enlarge the runway went on around the clock so that the German airlift to Norway could start in the spring of 1943. The project provided work for many Danes, mostly local people. Nevertheless, some still looked askance at anyone who would support Nazi Germany against little Norway, even indirectly. The Norwegians' heroic struggle was followed closely by the Danes, who suffered from guilt over their country's failure to stand up to the occupying forces.

Gunnar and Luffe had taken turns watching the guard changes at the airfield. As far as they could see, there was a kind of slack period between about eleven and eleven-thirty at night, when guard coverage was relatively light. There would be just enough time then to come out of the woods, cross the runway, and reach the main office building, which was the target of their operation. The vital thing was to pick the moment so as to avoid being caught in the sweeping beam of the searchlight mounted on the control tower.

The main building was less than one hundred fifty feet from the control tower and the low hangar. The Germans had also turned a large gray building into a barracks, and that had to be taken into consideration as well.

They set out late, Lars and Gunnar using the same excuse as Luffe and Søren: They told their parents they were going to the rowing club to work on the shell. This went down easily. It was always an honor to have your son in the eight.

No one knew or cared what sort of excuse Otto Hvidemann had made. The main thing was to all be in place at the appointed time. And now here they were in the dark, on what they each felt was their first real operation. Somehow Søren had procured a stick of greasepaint, and they had camouflaged their faces with it. Their eyes were fixed on the runway and the sweeping cone of the searchlight. And on their watches.

Earlier Lars had been to see Rosen. He was puttering around his room in his Chinese silk dressing gown, farther away from the real world and the war than suited Lars— today, anyway. He'd have liked to take Rosen into his confidence, to tell him about his lurking fears and uncomfortable twinges of doubt. As Rosen had once said, "Life is so short, Lars Balstrup, that we can't afford to waste much time."

Not that Lars felt this was a waste of time. But if worse came to worst, however trivial the operation might seem, it could be an unpardonable waste of life. Could be. He had said nothing to Rosen, however, maybe to spare the unworldly organist, who surely had anxieties of his own.

Lars glanced at the others. Gunnar seemed to have grown with this mission. Suddenly his authority had gained an objective: He had a job to do. Søren seemed particularly high-strung, just waiting; it was hard to say what for. Luffe was paler than usual. Otto was carrying an old-fashioned backpack. . . . What did they really know about Otto? Nothing, except that he worked at least eight hours a day in the brick-yard, his father was dead, and he had single-handedly stolen a Luger from the occupying forces. He had passed his initiation test with flying colors. He hadn't budged an inch, even after both Søren and Gunnar had perhaps let a little extra time go by. But when Lars looked at the palms of Otto's hands later, there was blood on them.

"OK," whispered Gunnar now. "As we agreed, Søren stays here on the outskirts of the woods, with the flashlight. If there are any problems, he'll signal twice."

Søren nodded.

"Lars is our lookout man. He'll cover the landing-strip area and keep an eye out for Søren's signal. Luffe, Hvidemann, and I will go in and work as planned—fast and without any fuss. Is that understood?"

Everyone nodded.

"We all depend on one another," whispered Gunnar, "the same as when we're in the boat. If one fails, we all go down."

"Only with the difference," added Søren quietly, "that we aren't doing this for medals. Or trophies."

"No. We're doing it for the honor of the town—and the country," whispered Gunnar.

He glanced at Luffe, who was carrying the rolled-up posters.

Lars checked his watch. Somewhere a propeller whirred. Behind the big hangar an airplane was warming up. In the darkness broken by the sweeping blue searchlight, the sound was menacing.

Lars knew Gunnar had the pistol in his inside pocket. It was a comforting thought, yet he could see that Søren had a point. You didn't steal license plates, caps, and flags with a Luger. If they were unlucky enough to be caught in possession of a screwdriver and crowbar, who cared? But what would the Germans do to a group of Danes breaking and entering, armed with a German gun? Gunnar had asked and answered that question, not mincing his words, when he, Otto, and Lars were practicing with the gun in the meadow behind the brickyard.

"They'll jail us—maybe in Germany. Just as long as you're clear about that." He aimed at a small sack containing slag. "Does it scare you, little brother?"

Lars hadn't looked at him when he answered. "Yes, Gunnar, it scares the hell out of me."

Gunnar made an adjustment, fired, and missed. Lars tried too, but missing didn't bother him. "If there has to be shooting," he said frankly, "I'm not the one to do it."

"What about you, Hvidemann?" Gunnar had asked. "Can you fire a gun?"

Otto took the pistol, released the safety catch, and blasted a large hole in the sack.

"Yes," he said. "I can."

On the stroke of eleven they dashed across the runway, bending low, dropping to the ground when the pale blue cone of the searchlight swept over the asphalt, then sprinting on again over to the airfield building, where they flattened themselves breathlessly against the wall.

Lars noticed that his breathing hurt, like some new, foreign body inside his own. He looked at Luffe, whose hands were shaking as he fumbled with the keys he had made especially for this occasion. Otto was holding the posters now.

Gunnar peered around the corner. There was a light in the barracks. They could even hear music.

"Get a move on, Luffe," he whispered impatiently.

Luffe looked up. "They're playing Benny Goodman," he said.

Gunnar rolled his eyes heavenward.

Luffe crawled over to the lock and tried the first key. It didn't fit. The next three were no use either.

Lars caught sight of a solitary German guard strutting around with a dog on a leash.

"I can't figure it out," muttered Luffe. "This is supposed to be a master key, for God's sake!"

Gunnar's face was moist with sweat. When Luffe began trying his homemade keys once again, it was too much for Gunnar. "OK, let's clear out," he said. He mopped his chin dry and took hold of Luffe.

Lars caught Gunnar's arm. The guard had stopped.

"Wait," whispered Gunnar.

Luffe swore the keys were usually one hundred percent reliable.

Lars watched the guard intently. The man had a rifle over his shoulder. It must be loaded with live ammunition. And the dog. A single wrong movement, just one . . .

"Keep clear," whispered Gunnar. "And follow me."

Otto took a big step back, swung his foot, and kicked the door in.

They stared at the door, which had flown open, and then at Otto, who walked in.

"Well, I'll be damned!" muttered Gunnar.

The building was not particularly big, two hundred square feet at most. It contained a desk, eight chairs, and an unlocked closet.

A picture of the führer hung on the wall. He was staring down at them with his usual hysterical expression.

"Everyone knows what to do," whispered Gunnar. Luffe was already painting pimples and spectacles on Hitler's face.

As they had arranged before setting out, Lars took up his lookout position outside. Gunnar soon had the first poster tacked up. He and Luffe worked rapidly, while Lars watched the guard and his dog. It may work out yet, he told himself. Then I'll be back home in the safety of the rectory, with my father asleep and my mother darning socks. Safe under my quilt. And will I ever be happy tomorrow!

The telephone on the desk began to ring. Luffe and Gunnar stared at it.

Reacting involuntarily, Lars shot into the building and closed the door.

"What are we going to do?" he groaned.

Luffe stared at the telephone and put his hands over his ears. Gunnar was shuffling his feet. He bit his lip.

"We damn well have to answer it, Gunnar," called Lars.

Gunnar pulled the plug out of the wall. A brief second passed, a brief second during which Lars saw a picture like a still from a film. Everything frozen: Irene standing in the school yard; Rosen looking at his little watercolors sent by the girl in Hildesheim; his own mother and father out in the garden, hauling the Danish flag down.

"*Out!*" shouted Luffe. "Everyone out, for heaven's sake!"

They packed up with lightning speed. Lars opened the door just as Søren's warning signal flashed in the dark.

He closed the door again.

Gunnar stared at him, dumbstruck. "What on earth are you doing?"

"Søren's signaling."

Gunnar chewed his knuckles. Then they saw Otto dousing the inside of the building with kerosene from a big can.

"Otto!" shouted Lars.

Luffe flung the door open, and everything happened very fast after that. Three soldiers were already on their way over from the barracks, with several more following. The sound of Benny Goodman's clarinet mingled with the howl of a siren.

Luffe tripped in the dark and brought Gunnar down with him. They were up again in a moment, heading for the outskirts of the woods.

Lars, however, stood staring at Otto, who struck a match and dropped it, then got a good grip on Lars and dragged him away.

Within seconds the whole building went up in flames.

Lars felt the hard asphalt like something trying to force itself up between his legs. His sense of unreality grew. The dogs barking, the ugly screech of the siren howling on and on, the voices in the dark.

They found their bicycles. Søren was shouting something or other. Now pedal hard. Downhill, out on the path. Gunnar and Søren first, then Luffe, with Lars behind them. And bringing up the rear on his clumsy delivery bike, Otto Hvidemann the arsonist.

Half an hour later Lars and Otto were at the brewery, utterly exhausted. Søren and Luffe had left in separate directions, and Gunnar had disappeared toward home with a resigned shake of his head when he saw Lars and Otto racing off through town.

Lars looked at Otto, his eyes shining.

"We did it, Otto," he said. "We damn well did it!"

Otto nodded with a hint of a smile and gazed out at the big brewery yard, where there were five piles of dray-horse droppings.

"Come on," he said quietly.

He negotiated the brewery as if he were at home there. They mounted a steep flight of iron steps, passing the long bottling shed. Up, up, around and around, until Otto stopped right at the top, in a cold room full of valves, nozzles, knobs, and gauges.

"What are we doing here?" Lars asked, smiling.

Otto went over to two large handles protruding from the wall. Each had a pale blue porcelain knob on its end. Otto needed to stand on tiptoe to reach them. He grasped them in his dirty hands, turned around just for a second, and gave Lars a resolute look. Then he pulled. Immediately a shrill wail broke out. The factory sirens filled the air with a two-note victory cry that made the hair rise on the back of Lars's neck.

Otto let go of the handles and fished a cigarette butt out of his breast pocket, lighting it expertly. Lars sat down on the floor in a state of bewilderment.

Outside, the night was black as pitch. Somewhere else in the dark, a building was on fire. A modest contribution, perhaps, but nonetheless a sign of success.

S E V E N

Lars earned himself a little extra cash by weeding the kitchen garden twice a week. His mother had had the bright idea of making the family self-sufficient, and she struck up various arrangements, more or less amounting to barter, with the butcher and two local part-time farmers. What they got from her in exchange was never discussed, but Lars had a feeling that Father, Son, and Holy Ghost had long ago been converted into some kind of currency and traded in. Rosen, who claimed to approve of anything rational so long as it didn't entail callousness, had once hinted that when Farmer Kjaer was laid to rest in consecrated ground, in the fall of 1941, even his nearest and dearest were surprised, in view of the fact that Kjaer was not a member of the Church of Denmark. But his wife was, so the old farmer joined the church posthumously, for the price of half a pig. As Reverend Balstrup observed when they were eating the pickled pork the following Christmas, "It does no harm to the churchyard, the good Lord, or the pig."

The war had induced a certain sense of pragmatism. Long forgotten crafts and skills had reemerged, and Lars, with growing astonishment, had heard his mother say, Yes, it was all very dreadful, Hitler and Goebbels and Mussolini and the news you heard over the radio from London, yet it was as if a new spirit had come over the town. The spirit of the old days. People were like one big family. They pulled closer together and helped one another out. Even some residents of the Sunset Home, long considered hopeless cases, seemed stirred into action. It was rumored that Mr. Jorgensen, a retired teacher who hadn't been able to walk or remember his own name for years, could now be found actually standing outside the local newspaper offices every morning, reading the latest war bulletins. His mind became clearer with each day, and he astonished the nursing staff by reeling off the names of eighty-five German and fifteen Russian towns at suppertime. It was a fact that the war had given a number of people a new lease on life.

"So we ought to be grateful to the Germans?" Lars had asked his mother.

"Not grateful, but there's no denying they've put certain things in their proper place, and we can't afford to complain."

"That's not the same as simply letting things slide," Lars had persisted, thinking it was about time to lay out the terrain properly. This conversation took place in the spring, the day they were cleaning the cellar, surrounded by large quantities of canning jars arranged in alphabetical order. His mother's storeroom was jammed. You had to admit that Mrs. Balstrup's managerial skills deserved a larger family.

"Has it never occurred to you," said his mother, lining the shelves with new paper, "that Hitler might well win this war? Haven't you ever stopped to think this isn't necessarily a passing phase, and that in time we may have to accept being part of the greater German Reich and adapt to it?"

Rosen usually helped with the cellar cleaning. It was a pleasant occasion. He and the minister's wife would sing duets in Swedish. Now he appeared behind her; she hadn't realized he was there.

"That thought," he said, out loud, but apparently talking to himself, "is one we simply cannot entertain."

Three hours later, when his mother had left the cellar to set to work on the church bazaar in the parish hall, Lars could hear Rosen puttering about among the jars of berry preserves and singing in Swedish: "Who can sail without a wind? Who can row without an oar? Who can part from faithful friends and never weep for days of yore?"

Lars had found the hoe and was at work among the potatoes when Gunnar came walking across the lawn, wearing his wiliest expression. The incident at the airfield had been two days ago, and the St. Petri Group had not met since. However, Lars had an idea that Gunnar and in particular Søren had a whole chicken yard full of bones to pick with a certain Otto Hvidemann.

"Well, well, nice to see you working!" said Gunnar.

Lars leaned on his hoe.

His brother glanced around and then produced a copy of the local paper from under his shirt. "Want a look?"

Lars smiled. "Sure."

Not a big story, but well placed. Lars read it and felt excitement spread through him like a widening smile.

> Boyish pranks directed against the German troops have now assumed such proportions as to cause the police concern. Apart from the usual acts of vandalism, the theft of road signs and license plates, the town has recently seen the occurrence of more serious offenses verging on sabotage. The police wish to warn the perpetrators—

Lars stopped. The word *sabotage* shot through him like a lightning bolt, warming, exciting, scorching him. He looked at Gunnar, who was rocking back and forth on the balls of his feet with an expression of exaggerated innocence.

"Terrific!" laughed Lars. "Us, in the paper! What a shame we can't tell anyone!"

"You know, we can't even think of that," Gunnar said, in tones that surprised Lars. "And what's more, I think Søren's right. In the future we must insist on very, very different conduct from Otto Hvidemann. And strict discipline. That performance he put on—"

"—is what got us into the paper." Lars went back to hoeing potatoes.

Gunnar followed him at a little distance. Lars could tell from his voice that he wasn't really angry.

"Yes, but then again he could have landed us in serious trouble, and the idea is *not*, as a matter of fact, to get into the local paper."

"Isn't it? Isn't that part of it? Showing the Germans that not all Danes are happy about the occupation, or willing to put up with it? Showing them we'll be damned if we'll stand for having them here?"

"Lars. It so happens I can remember the look on your face when we were out there on the airfield."

Lars sighed noisily.

"You're prepared to fight the Germans," said Gunnar quietly. "But are you prepared to pay the price too?"

"What do you mean?"

"I mean that if those fat Germans hadn't been spending a pleasant evening in their barracks, enjoying the radio and a few beers, some of us might not have come home. On account of Otto."

Lars dropped the hoe and walked a little way off. Gunnar followed him and put his hands on Lars's shoulders.

"Look, I'll talk to him," said Lars. "But you have to realize, Otto's sort of—different. Impulsive."

Gunnar burst out laughing. "Impulsive! He's pure dynamite!"

Then they were both laughing.

"To think of him lugging two gallons of kerosene along, all on his own. . . ."

Lars looked at his older brother, suddenly feeling absurdly protective. Nothing bad must happen to Gunnar. Every imaginable means must be used to prevent such a thing. Not a hair of his angelic head must be harmed.

"The worst part," Gunnar went on, serious again, "is the drug it injects into your bloodstream."

Lars glanced up. "What drug?"

"Didn't you feel it? When you were coming home?" Gunnar looked away dreamily. "My blood was racing along like a Norwegian mountain torrent. The excitement, the sense of being so alive . . ."

Lars nodded. Yes, that was exactly what it had been like. "When Otto set off the sirens in the brewery . . . I'll never forget that," Lars said.

Gunnar grinned. "I knew it was you two. It gave me goose bumps all over. I was talking to Luffe. He's hardly slept since. He's experimenting with something new, and yesterday he went to the library in town and bumped into Suckerfish there—you know, that thin, sinister-looking gestapo man." Gunnar smiled broadly. "But Luffe just thought of the airfield building going up in flames while the sirens were wailing. He was laughing the whole way home."

Lars could just imagine. It was odd, though—he'd met the gestapo man in the library himself. Oh, well, maybe Suckerfish was a bookworm.

Gunnar blew his nose. "OK, Lars," he said. "There's a meeting tomorrow. I've got to go now—I'm supposed to visit an aunt with Irene's family. Sounds thrilling, doesn't it?"

Lars nodded and picked up his hoe.

———

What people in town called the shanty settlement consisted of ten blocks of workers' dwellings built in the late nineteenth century on land behind the Kolstrup Brickyard. There were usually a great many men at home, unemployed, sitting or standing by their front doors or on the street corners where the children played. It was hard to get work in the middle of summer, unless you could find day labor of some kind. Most of those who did have regular jobs worked either in the brick-yard or the brewery.

Lars left his bicycle outside Number 18. He had been by there once before, just to see what it looked like. He waited for a moment, watching a little girl with a cup of soapy water. She was blowing a big soap bubble when the front door behind her opened.

The woman was in her midthirties, elegantly dressed, pretty in a natural sort of way. She looked like a model in a fashion magazine, more because of the way she carried herself than her clothes themselves. She wore quite a lot of makeup, but she didn't appear cheap.

"Looking for anyone?" She smiled rather distantly at Lars, in a way he later thought of as courteous.

"Yes," he said. "Does someone called Otto Hvidemann live here?"

Her expression suddenly became less forthcoming, a little guarded. But she was still smiling as she said, "Oh, yes. Otto's my son."

Lars took an involuntary step backward. If he had tried to imagine Otto's mother, she wouldn't in a million years have looked like this woman. She didn't actually look like anyone's mother.

He introduced himself and saw her raise her thin, painted eyebrows slightly.

"Balstrup—I never knew Otto had such fine friends!"

Perhaps there was a subtle irony in her words. Or was it just a manner she'd adopted? A protective device that helped to tighten her mouth and make her eyes a little hard?

"Otto's down by the fjord with his sisters." She smiled again and walked toward the road, turning to look down and check if the seams of her stockings were straight. They were—straight as a ruler.

The next moment she was gone.

It was late afternoon. Midsummer in Denmark. The fjord was dead calm. Blue as the sky it mirrored. Beautiful as the day it was made. Peace and quiet everywhere, thought Lars, as if Mother Nature were sweetly napping. A little way out in the fjord, Otto was walking through the shallow water in a skimpy undershirt and bathing trunks, pulling a flat-bottomed rowboat after him. In it, his two sisters, aged six and eight, were busy looking down into the water as though searching for something. Lars was able to step closer without being noticed. He could have watched Otto for hours, absorbing the scene the way a traveler on a train in a foreign country absorbs the images passing by the window.

Now he saw what they were doing: They were gathering mussels. The little girls splashed water at Otto, who just smiled in his shy, private way and went on searching.

Soon he pulled them and the boat back in again, and Lars waved to him.

Otto did not react to the newspaper report. Maybe he had no interest in that sort of thing.

The Hvidemanns' place consisted of two small rooms and a little kitchen. The lavatories were out in the yard. Lars tried to act as if he were used to being in homes where the wallpaper was hanging off the walls, but he could see that Otto was uncomfortable having him there. He took the smaller of his sisters off to put dry clothes on her.

Lars waited in the living room, where there were photographs of Otto's father and mother and other people Lars didn't know. Three packs of English cigarettes and a bottle of cognac were on a shelf above the table.

The elder girl came and joined him. Her name was Kylle.

"It's wash day today," she said, sucking a piece of candy. "Otto has to wash our clothes."

Otto appeared in the doorway, holding the smaller girl by the hand. They were very like each other, with the same vulnerable, slightly wary expression. Not at all like their mother, thought Lars. But perhaps she had once looked like that too.

"I really just came to show you the newspaper story," said Lars, smiling.

Otto sent the little girls outside. "Find Monty," he told them, and looked at Lars. "That's the next-door neighbors' rooster."

Kylle reminded Otto that it was wash day. Otto nodded and closed the door. Lars didn't really know where to begin. It would have been easier on neutral ground.

"The thing is, Otto—you see—Gunnar was saying that maybe next time—well, you know, first we ought to agree on what we're going to do. . . ."

"Mmph?"

Lars smiled. "Well, strictly speaking, we didn't agree to anything about burning the whole building down."

Otto looked away. It's possible he knows perfectly well what I'm getting at, thought Lars. He just goes his own way. "So things worked out OK that time, but . . ."

Otto was still gazing at some point in the distance when he finally spoke. "We should have taken out the barracks. The big one."

Lars stared at him, baffled. "For heaven's sake, it was crammed full of Germans!"

Otto returned his stare, with his customary expression of vulnerability that spoke of something else.

Lars cleared his throat and went to the door. He was at a loss. What on earth could Otto mean? The barracks! Did he wish all those people had been burned alive? All the men sitting there listening to Benny Goodman?

On the other hand, they *were* the occupying power.

"Otto . . . ," he said, "you'll remember about next time?"

Otto nodded.

Lars opened the door and went out. There was something about the air in there that didn't agree with him. Not that the place had a bad smell, because it didn't, and it wasn't stuffy. It was more an oppressive feeling, something he couldn't put into words.

He was just opening the lock on his bike when Otto came out with a brown paper bag.

"I thought you and your family might like some mussels."

Lars looked at the bag and then at Otto.

"Thanks," he said, taking the bag. "Thanks a lot, Otto."

E I G H T

As a rule, the German military band marched from Østergade down Algade to Jernbanegade and then all the way around town. Although it was generally a peaceful enough procession, most people saw it as another reminder of German power: a noisy one conveyed by drums, brass, and the tramp of marching feet. The town had to put up with it every afternoon.

You could almost set your watch by the smug little drum major, who had very likely left a job as a salesman in a men's clothing store in a south German country town where he was an absolute zero to strut at the head of the assembled troops—swinging a baton to boot.

Lars hated this spectacle, partly because some of his fellow countrymen obviously enjoyed the music and partly because the marching and the whole show symbolized all the perversity of the war, with the Nazi banner replaced by the familiar German emblem of the glowering eagle, paraded around town like some holy relic.

Today, there was no way Lars and Gunnar could avoid the show. The note they'd had from Søren and Luffe told them to be outside the German headquarters at four-thirty exactly, when the commandant and three noncommissioned officers stood ready to click their heels together as the stout clothing salesman and his band strode past.

There were always a certain number of spectators on hand at four-thirty. Maybe they just had nothing else to do. Lars saw the notorious Junkersen from their school. He was deep in friendly conversation with Suckerfish, who always wore a long black raincoat. The teacher's forefinger was wagging rhythmically in front of the gestapo man's face, like a metronome keeping time with the music. He was smiling pleasantly, and for all anyone knew a beautiful picture postcard was unfolding in Junkersen's imagination, showing him standing at the top of the steps where the commandant now stood, attired in black boots, black uniform, and black visor cap. A vision terrifying enough to make anyone shudder. Junkersen's greasy suit didn't have quite the same effect on his students, but that day might come, as he had pointed out to Lars when Lars had run into him in the corridor one morning. His back half-turned to the teacher, he had been calling out to a bunch of boys, "Heil Hitler, Heil Hitler! Ever see anybody look much littler?"

Junkersen had taken firm hold of his arm. "I'll have none of that here in school, Lars Balstrup. Is that clear?"

Now Lars looked away from Junkersen and Suckerfish, turned to Gunnar, and suggested leaving. But Gunnar wanted to stay where Søren and Luffe had said to meet. Then they saw Kirsten walking down the street with her father, the fat doctor. She looked good in her tailored pale gray suit and little pillbox hat. Kirsten never wore hand-me-down clothes. Her hair was pinned up, and the little hat was tilted prettily on her head. She came up the street with a spring in her step. Lars imagined her on the red gravel of the tennis court: her white skirt and her brown knees, her elegant shots— backhand, forehand, serve.

"You lucky devil, you!" muttered Gunnar, bowing politely and putting his hands behind his back as if they weren't worthy to be offered to so superb a creature. She smiled broadly and said it was funny, them running into each other here. What was so funny about it? Well, she was only just back from Skagen, and her mother was still there. "So Daddy and I will have a bit of peace and quiet while it lasts!" They all three laughed.

At that moment the band thumped its way by, and Kirsten's voice was drowned out by the noise. As the commandant at the top of the steps was raising his arm in the rigid Nazi salute, a rag-doll effigy five feet long dropped from the roof and dangled in front of the startled officers' noses. The effigy had a head, arms, and legs, and was dressed in a salmon pink bra and girdle. Its face was the spitting image of Adolf Hitler.

The music gradually died away. Lars glanced at Junkersen and Suckerfish. The teacher's cheeks were red, flushed with indignation. However, the gestapo man merely let his glance wander blankly over the Danes assembled on the sidewalk.

Kirsten had quit her role of fashion model and was staring openmouthed at her father. The fat doctor was staring grimly ahead.

An unusual sense of confusion passed through the German ranks. "I'm afraid we have to go now," said Gunnar, tugging at Lars's sleeve. Lars nodded to Kirsten.

"Lars," she called after him, "will I see you soon?"

She stood on tiptoe, which wasn't really called for, but as he thought about it he realized that she always did stand slightly on her toes, and she was always arching her neck a little, or hopping restlessly from foot to foot.

He turned the corner after Gunnar. I'll write, thought Lars. I'll write her a letter saying it won't work. Saying she's too good to—to be trifled with. Let alone the fact that they had never really talked much and he'd never promised her anything. He hadn't even promised himself anything.

Gunnar was standing with his back to a wall, grinning all over his face. "Good work, Luffe . . . and Søren too. That's the way!"

Lars shook his head and smiled lightly. Somehow he couldn't get the picture of Junkersen, Suckerfish, and poor little suntanned Kirsten out of his mind.

The meeting began on the dot, as usual. Only one item was on the agenda: Otto Hvidemann.

Their laughter at the show Søren and Luffe had put on was now forgotten. Otto was a serious matter. He sat at the end of the table in his dark blue work clothes, without any real idea what he was being accused of. He was fascinated by the big loft and occupied himself by looking around the place.

Gunnar repeated his warnings about the importance of sticking to what they had arranged ahead of time. "We have to insist on strict discipline," he explained.

There was silence. Lars gave Otto a small encouraging smile. Søren asked whether Otto Hvidemann had anything to say.

"Mm, well, yes," murmured Otto, after a pause. "The Germans have a store of arms in the pump house down by the harbor. I thought we might be able to break in. Then we could get ahold of submachine guns *and* ammunition."

Søren and Gunnar stared at him incredulously. Even Luffe's usual silly grin disappeared. The place was so quiet you could hear the church clock creaking and ticking down below, and the swallows twittering around the tower.

Gunnar tilted his chair backward and bit the stem of his pipe.

Søren looked at Gunnar, tense as a spring. "Has insanity broken out here, or what?"

Gunnar looked back at his friend, with an expression on his face as if he had neither heard nor understood the question.

"Submachine guns!" Søren rose to his feet, prowled ominously around Otto's chair, and then stationed himself behind it.

The others still had a vivid image of the dangling rag doll with Hitler's face. But Otto didn't. He'd hardly have understood, and indeed, why should he?

Ever since early childhood, Luffe had had a slight speech impediment, a tendency to stammer when he was excited. Gunnar was lighting his pipe when Luffe exclaimed, "S-s-submachine guns . . ."

Søren brought the flat of his hand down on the table. "I've had about enough of this." He pointed at Otto. "Is *he* in charge now, Gunnar?"

Otto seemed bewildered as Lars remarked that you could bet the guns weren't left lying around for anyone to march in and walk off with, just like that.

"We damn well aren't going to walk off with so much as a single submachine gun," Søren shouted. "Insanity *must* have broken out here! What on earth would we use the damn things for, anyway?"

Otto looked at him. "For shooting," he explained, with the kind of artless logic that would always leave him and Søren worlds apart.

"It's too dangerous," Gunnar said calmly. "Much too dangerous."

"But Gunnar," began Luffe, "s-s-subm-m-machine guns?"

"I said it's too dangerous, Luffe."

"It's a one-man job," said Otto.

The words hung in the air like a soap bubble. Before anyone could burst the bubble, Otto went on, "I was thinking the best time to do it would be during the songfest by the fjord."

Gunnar took the pipe out of his mouth. "The community songfest? Yes, but that's Regatta Day. . . ."

Otto nodded. "Which means the whole town will be empty."

There was another longish pause while they all thought about that.

Lars leaned over the table and said with some reluctance, "It—it does seem too dangerous to me. A one-man job, Otto? Who'd keep watch for you?"

"But a s-s-subm-m-machine gun!" breathed Luffe.

Gunnar's glance flickered slightly. "We could vote on it," he said in a subdued voice.

Luffe's hand shot up like a rocket. "I'm in f-f-favor!"

Søren smiled at him and put his own hand up too.

Lars looked at them for some time and then said, "I'm against. Dead against!"

They looked at Gunnar, who swallowed. "I'm against too," he said. "It's too risky."

Lars loved him for saying that.

Then Otto's hand went up.

Luffe pointed at him like a little boy pointing at a balloon in a carnival stall. "Three against two, Gunnar," he said. "Three against two."

Lars gave Otto's sleeve a tug. "Think it over, Otto. Please."

Otto was looking not at him, but at some point a long way from the church. Maybe he was already out there in the dark pump house, following his own strategy, carrying out his own plan. Without the help of any rag-doll effigies whatsoever.

N I N E

The day before the regatta and the big summer songfest down by the fjord, Lars decided to wander around for a while after supper. It was the end of July. He would take his bike and ride around wherever he felt like. The evening was heavy with rain, the air saturated with thousands of tiny drops. In spite of the season, Lars sensed the unmistakable coming of fall.

In September of last year, as summer drew to a close, he'd made a new and disturbing discovery. He had mentioned it to Rosen, who did not seem surprised, but merely said it was to be welcomed as a sign of maturity. Was he speaking from experience—maybe bitter experience? And how could melancholy be a sign of maturity? Was there some natural law of sadness? Rosen said there was great beauty in melancholy: Things didn't fit together in so straightforward a way, and here as elsewhere yin and yang were closely interwoven.

Lars was not at all sure he understood this, but he felt it deep inside him, like a melody in a minor key. He caught himself sitting with closed eyes just to let it carry him along as time passed by. Carry him down a long lazy river, drifting . . . parting. The word echoed in his mind like an alarm call. He saw pictures of locomotives slowly beginning to move, ferries casting off, people waving good-bye with tears running down their cheeks. Parting. Disaster. Unrequited love.

By accident, he had found himself sitting opposite her in a shelter one day when an air-raid warning had taken the town by surprise. As a rule that meant nothing; you just went sedately downstairs into the shelter and waited decorously. There were about twenty people there, a random selection of Danes perched as if waiting for a bus. Then Lars caught sight of Irene in the dark room. She was sitting with her purse on her lap, smiling wanly at him. That was all right, then. She could have been watching him for some time, because he was the last to come running in before the door was closed.

They were sitting too far from each other to carry on a conversation, so Lars just nodded. Suppose the town was bombed to bits? Suppose all the walls came down and not a stone was left standing? The idea was like a dreadful dream, but all the same it gave him a warm, exhilarated feeling. Just that small handful of survivors after a final bombardment.

They'd grieve together. In his mind another feeling mingled with the grieving and the melancholy autumn sensation. They looked at each other. Lars was glad they couldn't talk. It made everything so much easier—he never knew what to say. So he just gestured, turning the palms of his hands up. She smiled. A sweet, slightly teasing smile, as if to say, Never mind all that nonsense.

The next moment the all-clear sounded. On the way up to the light of day, she said, "Mr. Balstrup, the great fortune-teller." In a deep voice.

"Oh, yes," he sighed. "That's the trouble with being able to see into the future."

She laughed hilariously, but was serious the next moment. He took her hand and turned it over. Right there in the middle of the street, with the remains of the town lying in ruins around them, yellow smoke drifting among the rubble, the sound of a siren in the distance. A vast pillar of smoke swaying in the wind a long way off, the sky red as blood. And an unmistakable smell of artificial coffee.

"Can you see anything, you idiot?"

He sighed. Her hand was warm and dry, and a little larger than you might expect. They were standing so close together that their foreheads almost touched, which wasn't really necessary. He let the tip of his forefinger trace the lines of her hand. The line of destiny. Their knees bumped. He felt a brief electric shock below the waist. I'll just stay here, he thought, I'll stay until they come and carry me away. Until we're fossilized, turned to stone, washed away by the sea of time. And in a thousand years a little boy will pick us up.

He'll stand on a beach in Argentina and look at our fossils merged together. Two human beings, a single destiny.

He crossed the square and cycled through the nearest residential neighborhood, where a blackbird was singing after the rain.

"Tomorrow," he murmured. "It's tomorrow. I won't sleep tonight: I'll wait up and watch the dawn."

"Feeling nervous, little brother?" He remembered Gunnar's bright angel face as the dinner table had been cleared. "You just attend to your little tiller, and the rest of us will leave those lowland farmers far behind."

Reverend Balstrup had gone into the living room and turned the radio on. It was time for the BBC broadcast from London.

After the race—a voice inside Lars had whispered as he left the house without having coffee with the others—after the race, when the trophy's presented, Gunnar will want to gather his nearest and dearest around him. All his school friends, Søren and Luffe, Mother and Father. He'll stand on a chair, and there'll be a thick emphatic line drawn to mark the day, a point of intersection in autumn colors. A proclamation in silver. While darkness falls over the fjord, not so very far away, on the other side of the water, a small solitary figure will be venturing into the heavily guarded pump house. Fate. Destiny . . .

He turned left. Oh, for heaven's sake, Otto, don't!

Then, suddenly, he saw her. She was standing with her back to him, waiting while her family's terrier, Winston, sniffed around a lamppost.

Exactly a month ago, just before Midsummer Day, he had run into her at the same place. Completely by chance. On that occasion he had risen in the bike seat and pedaled as hard as he could, passing her with a brief "Hi!" But what had he imagined he could do? Hang around gaping at her like a Peeping Tom? Exactly!

She looked up and smiled. Lars kept calm and slowly rode closer. Come on, he told himself, behave yourself, think up some kind of lie.

"I—I have a message for you from Gunnar. He couldn't come himself. It's about tomorrow. He said you were to meet at the place you'd fixed."

This feeble story hung in the air between them like a limp paper chain.

She raised her brows, which were broad and dark, not thin and plucked.

"So? You came all the way over here just to tell me that?"

"Well, not exactly. I have to go on to see Luffe and take him a . . . a mechanical pencil."

Oh, aren't we just doing brilliantly, said the officious little voice at the back of his head. A mechanical pencil, of all things!

She looked at her dog. "Luffe? He lives at the other end of town."

"That's right, but he's—he's visiting a friend over this way."

Idiot. Idiot. Idiot. It was sweet of her not to laugh.

"Are you nervous about tomorrow?"

He looked directly at her. "Me? No . . . not a bit. We're sure to win."

She laughed doubtfully.

"Are *you* nervous?" He made his voice sound light.

"Am I nervous? Well, I don't have to go out there and row."

Lars looked up in the air, forcing a smile.

"No, but—well, Gunnar told me ages ago." He pointed meaningfully at her ring finger.

She looked away as if something had struck her on the head. The wind ruffled her hair. Then she looked back at him, but she didn't say anything, just looked. That autumn feeling.

He was home half an hour later. Sitting in his room, staring at his globe. Down in the living room his father was singing a song that started "Comrade, comrade of the sun . . ."

He could have said something else. Why hadn't they gone on talking? But Lars had only looked at her little fox terrier, who for some reason or other hadn't said anything either. And when he turned the corner she was still standing in the same spot, staring down at the ground. Or was she watching him go?

T E N

About a thousand people had gathered on the banks of the isthmus that extended into the fjord like a flat tongue. The dannebrog, the Danish national flag, was waving, and everyone had just finished the second to the last song before the race. Now the girls' chorus, in red-and-white robes, took up the final one. Their clear voices rang out over the water, rising on the wind and settling over the land, filling the crowd with every word:

> "Not long ago we saw rain fall,
> The storm wind lashed the wood.
> Over the hedges the weed seeds all
> Drifted, settled where they would.
> Our necks are bowed, our mouths are dumb,

Through all the seasons' stages:
Within these groves, joy once did come
Where now the tempest rages."

Lars stood beside Søren, who was singing at the top of his lungs. The words, the swell of the voices, and the beautiful surroundings gave the song its full force. It suggested burning flames of defiance. Søren was wearing a white shirt and a blue tie. His eyes were shining. Lars thought how often Gunnar said, Søren's my best friend; you can always rely on him.

When the singing was over, they joined the others, who were getting the shell ready.

A letter had arrived for Filip Rosen that morning. Mother said it was from Germany. Rosen had not come down to the songfest. That in itself was disturbing. Lars hadn't been able to speak to the organist, because Rosen had kept his door closed.

Down by the boat they were discussing the wind and the tide. A boy called Axel, who was in Gunnar's class, had been over to take a look at the competition and reported that there were two new men in the other eight.

"That's lucky for us," said Axel optimistically.

"No," replied Gunnar. "They're from the Speedy Boat Club, those two new men, and they row like Vikings. We can't afford to relax for a second. And don't forget we've promised the principal we'll win!"

As always, Gunnar was good at inspiring his crew; his voice was almost frenzied now as he urged them on in his usual prerace pep talk.

Lars went into the clubhouse, where Søren was changing. They looked gravely at each other.

Then Søren said, "I'm sorry about your brother."

Lars watched him fold his clothes into two neat piles. Outside, people were coming along to wish the pride and joy of the town good luck.

"What do you mean, sorry about him?"

Søren went over to Lars and spoke in a confidential tone. "The other day he showed me two silver rings he'd bought. You know, for him and Irene. . . ."

Lars turned away, pulling his shirt over his head.

"He was going to announce their engagement after the regatta, but now—"

"Now what?" asked Lars, feeling himself go both hot and cold at once.

Søren sighed and ran a comb through his hair in front of the mirror.

"Well, now the lady suddenly wants to wait—so there's poor old Gunnar left flat!"

Lars went to the door and looked intently at his hand as it pushed down on the handle. Judas, said the little voice.

The course was laid out so that the finish line was right inside the harbor basin. By now everyone who had come for the songfest had walked along the shore toward town. Most of them had brought sandwiches and were enjoying the fine weather and a welcome opportunity to have a good time. The dannebrog flew everywhere. Not a flagpole was without it.

Meanwhile the crew prepared for the race, stretching and

warming up. As cox, Lars had been shouting out a rhyme he made up during training—a nonsense verse that had so far worked pretty well. But once they had the boat in the water, Gunnar came over and put an arm around his shoulders.

"Lars, let me say whatever needs to be said today."

"But—will you have enough breath for that?"

"You bet I will." Gunnar looked thoughtfully at his hands. "And—oh, hell," he muttered. "I was really looking forward to today!"

Lars cleared his throat and glanced away.

"First of all, this business about Rosen, and then . . . well, you know we were going to get engaged?"

Lars nodded and muttered something or other both meaningless and incoherent.

"Well, now she suddenly says it's too soon. After almost two years."

Gunnar gazed across the water. Lars laid a hand on his back. There were a great many things angels didn't understand, that was a fact. What were they doing down here on earth anyway? Here among all the cheats and liars.

Gunnar glanced up quickly. "All the same," he said firmly, "we'll show those lowland farmers a thing or two."

Watching him head off to join the others, Lars told himself that was the very last time he'd ever go near the part of town where Irene lived.

The crack of the starter's pistol sounded, and the boats pulled away. For the first few minutes, the two eights stayed side by side; it seemed clear this would be a close race. In the other boat, the cox was shouting so hard he went white around the mouth. Lars didn't say a word; he just worked the tiller. But by the time they rounded the first buoy they were half a length behind.

"Gunnar," shouted Søren. "Gunnar, they're getting away from us, man!"

"Keep the rhythm steady!" Gunnar called back. "Keep stroke!"

They stepped up their rate by several strokes a minute. The change happened smoothly and imperceptibly, like a sports car steadily accelerating.

Soon after that Lars could see the harbor, where the light was fading now. People had gathered along the quay. Then Gunnar shouted, "Here we go, lads! What will we do with Göring? Come on, what will we do?"

Lars hadn't known about this last-minute plan, but now the crew shouted out their rhyme in a single hoarse, raucous voice. It was a primitive cry that almost brought the eight right up out of the water:

"First we grab old Göring
By his big fat calves.
Then we knock down Goebbels—
We don't do things by halves!"

The two boats were side by side. The lowland farmers had put on a spurt and were pulling desperately at their oars.

"We'll dangle Hitler from a rope
And right beside him Ribbentrop:
Look how stupid, all in line,
One, two, three, four Nazi swine!"

Coming down the final straight, they put everything they had into it.

Gunnar let out his last spare breath. "And one more time for Denmark!"

By now their rhythmic chant could be heard on land, and it set off a round of applause. There were tears in Gunnar's eyes. Like a crazy man, he carried the other seven along with him. The race was out of control now. Somehow the verse and the words and their joint determination carried the crew half a length ahead of their rivals, who seemed paralyzed.

Gunnar's boat crossed the finish line. The jubilation knew no bounds. People threw their hats in the air. Lars stared at the others. They were exhausted, pain and adrenaline and the lunacy of it all showing in their faces. Several of them were weeping.

Gunnar splashed water from the fjord on his face and waved to his family. He looked at Lars with a small shaky smile.

"Fantastic," whispered Lars. "That was fantastic, Gunnar—congratulations."

An hour later, night had fallen. A few hundred people, most of them young, sat on the left bank around a dying fire. The girls sang the song of Denmark: "Danish song is a fair young girl, humming as she walks through Denmark's house!"

Irene was sitting between Gunnar and his mother, who led the singing with a happy smile.

Luffe made his way over to Lars. His hands were wrapped in gauze. "How do you think it's going?" he asked quietly, looking across to the opposite bank. "Do you think he's still in there?"

Lars stared at the massive silhouette of the pump house.

An hour later only about twenty people were left. It was completely dark now, and only those sitting closest to the embers could see one another. The Reverend and Mrs. Balstrup had gone home. He had had an absent expression on his face. But she had kissed both Lars and Gunnar on the forehead, saying, "Have a nice time, boys. We're off now to see how our little organist is doing." In her experience, there was nothing in the world that couldn't be cured with a bandage, a little iodine, a cup of chamomile tea, or a good night's sleep. Nothing at all.

Most people had begun shivering in the cold when a hoarse siren wailed over the harbor and the fjord.

Lars felt it go right through him. Luffe happily let himself tumble backward, making the V sign with both hands.

Gunnar, however, stared fixedly at the opposite bank. Either his beautiful angel wings were invisible in the dark or he had lost them out there on the water.

Lars got up and walked a bit in the dark. Kirsten had been there earlier, but he wasn't interested in Kirsten. He didn't even take the trouble to pretend he was. Kirsten was a nuisance. Unfortunate, but true. All those beautiful songs, the friendly camp-fire mood, all their Danish patriotism. Where did the aggression come from? He kept seeing a peaceful picture before him: Otto pulling his sisters along in the rowboat, looking for mussels for dinner. In the same water where the two eights had just been competing ferociously—for a trophy, for pride, for honor.

It was after midnight before Lars went to bed. He was exhausted yet lay there for a long time, tossing and turning. He thought he could detect the sound of faint music somewhere in the house. "I'm hearing things," he muttered, but in a little while he put on his bathrobe and opened the door into the hallway. There was no doubt about it. Quietly, he went down past the back kitchen, the dining room, and the study, to the little hall that led to Rosen's room. The music became louder. It sounded like a violin and another stringed instrument. An odd sound. He hesitated briefly, then knocked discreetly. No reply.

"Rosen," he called. "It's me, Lars."

After a moment the door opened. The organist didn't look at him, just sat down in his armchair and stared into space. He had a glass in his hands. Red wine, perhaps.

Lars closed the door after him. He noticed at once that the little watercolors were gone. He looked at Rosen, who observed him with a blurred, distracted gaze.

"Gone," he said. "All gone. And . . . and I just sit here."

Lars sat down on the floor in front of him.

"Nothing very special about it in itself, I suppose," Rosen went on. "Nothing sensational."

His acceptance felt forced. Filip Rosen was clinging by

his fingertips to a philosophy and a way of life that seemed flimsier and less substantial by the moment.

"Is there anything you'd like to talk about, Rosen?"

"Talk about? Well, we are talking about it, aren't we? Even if there isn't anything to talk about. That's life. You see, Lars, I got—I received this today."

Rosen took it out of his jacket pocket. The yellow Jewish star, in the mail from Germany. "I daresay—I daresay I could be made to use this souvenir myself."

"Nina," whispered Lars tonelessly.

Rosen didn't answer, just looked away.

"Work camps, they're called. Some of them are in Poland, some in Czechoslovakia. Bubbi . . . the youngest of the family, he's only eight years old. And now he'll have to wear those striped clothes too, and be deloused, and have his head shaved. Like—like my Nina. Would you be kind enough to leave me alone now, Lars?"

Lars closed the door of the organist's room but stayed there, waiting tensely for the music to begin again. He felt a sense of something shaking, plaster peeling away, stone cracking, rafters falling.

There ought to be nothing left, he thought, nothing at all. Not even understanding. Only the black hole, the dark vacuum where we hang weightless, unable to touch wall, ceiling, or floor. In that vacuum we'll learn to accept, to put up with everything, to tap our feet when the German troops march through town in the afternoon. Turn a blind eye and deaf ear when they click their heels in church and give their orders.

We'll do as they wish. And we'll be patient and magnanimous, like good Christians and citizens of an occupied nation, seeing through the uniform to the human being underneath: the clothing salesman, the student surveyor, the minister's son.

Back in his room, he twirled the globe on his desk. Around and around went its continents, its oceans, its various regions. *Lebensraum,* the Germans called it, living space.

They were on the march everywhere now: El Alamein, North Africa, in the Caucasus. Two million German soldiers. Bombs over Iceland. Bombs all over the place.

"Are you asleep, Otto Hvidemann?" he whispered. "Or have you just woken up?"

He stood there for a little while, looking at his bed. Then he went out and down the hall to Gunnar's room. He knocked three times and opened the door. Gunnar's bed was empty. It was two-thirty in the morning. Lars got his shoes and went over to the church tower, his steps slow but determined. Up all those steps, around and around. Beyond the belfry, he saw a light. He approached cautiously, although the creaking old stairs, the crumbling floorboards, and worm-eaten banisters gave him away long before he arrived.

The big loft was lit by three candelabra. Gunnar sat at one end of the heavy oak table, fully dressed. The trophy was in the middle of the table. Lars sat down at the other end.

Gunnar didn't look at him; he just sat there. Are we all under a spell tonight? Lars wondered. He felt a cold shiver run through him. A moment later Gunnar looked up. The action seemed to require great energy, but his eyes were peaceful and serene. He nodded as if they had been talking for hours, right through the thick Flemish bond brickwork of the rectory.

"Yes," he murmured, "there it is. The trophy."

Lars said, "Rosen had a letter."

Gunnar nodded sadly.

"About his girlfriend in Hildesheim," Lars went on.

"They came to take her and her family away," said Gunnar. "To Theresienstadt, in Czechoslovakia. In trucks, lots of trucks, packed with people."

Lars looked at the grain of the wood in the old table. That was something else inherited from their pipe-smoking grandfather in Viborg. Dollerup Bakker, dead and buried long ago. It was said he now lay side by side with the poet Steen Steensen Blicher, and what more could a bishop ask?

"Do you understand any of this?" Lars asked.

Gunnar put his feet up on the table. He looked tired. In spite of the trophy, he looked like a beaten man.

"Luffe says the Germans are going to change the freight traffic schedule in September," he said. "His father works on the railroad."

"What's that got to do with us, or the town—or Rosen?" Lars tried to make eye contact with this strange new Gunnar.

"It's because of the airlift of materials to Norway they're planning. There'll be more troops coming through, heavier artillery, truckloads of tanks, and so on. And then later in the year, in winter, the freight schedule's going to be changed again—for one special convoy. They'll be using Fredericia as the rail junction. It'll be a long, long train carrying tanks, antiaircraft guns, that sort of thing. Like I said, they're beginning on this project in September. They'll be sealing off the rolling stock depot. It'll be full of freight cars—freight cars carrying explosives."

"Explosives?" repeated Lars in a whisper.

Gunnar nodded. "So far as we know."

Only now did Lars catch sight of the two silver rings lying in the candlelight.

"Am I to understand," asked Lars, "that we're through with license plates and caps and rag-doll dummies and posters?"

"Are you to understand?" repeated Gunnar. "Good heavens, there's nothing *to* understand."

"Er—have you mentioned all this to Søren?"

"I haven't mentioned it to anyone. I'm just stating facts."

Gunnar rose to his feet and walked slowly over to the corner where there were two old hassocks and a tall country-style chest of drawers.

He pulled open the top drawer and glanced at Lars, who came over. In the drawer lay a partly assembled submachine gun and a rifle with telescopic sights.

"Otto," whispered Lars. "Otto was here."

Gunnar nodded and closed the drawer.

"Yes," he said. "Otto was here."

FALL

1942

ELEVEN

Lars was waiting for Otto outside the brickyard. He came out alone, as before, wheeling his clumsy bike. He seemed pleased to see Lars. They went back to Otto's place, where it was wash day again. His mother wasn't often at home. Lars had once asked what she did and quickly realized the subject wasn't one Otto liked to discuss.

It had been difficult explaining to him that the St. Petri Group had to lie low for a while. The gestapo was making its presence felt more and more these days. Maybe that was just coincidence, or maybe it was part of preparations for the airlift.

Lars had twice come across Suckerfish in the library, and now he knew what the man was doing there: studying genealogies. He'd even been around to the vestry to borrow the parish registers. They knew from the national newspapers that important documents pertaining to Jewish Danes had been confiscated from the official records office in Copenhagen. The Germans wanted lists of all Jews living in Denmark, to see whether they had any links with the saboteurs. There were rumors that a large-scale raid to arrest Jews in Copenhagen would occur in the near future, and similar rumors were now spreading in the provinces. More than once Reverend Balstrup had hinted that it might be a good idea for Rosen to go and stay in Sweden for a while. So far his suggestion had fallen on deaf ears. The organist went about his work as usual. Each service he sat at the organ and watched the Germans take their places in the pews.

Everyone was waiting. It was like a game of chess, with the chessmen coming closer and closer to one another one square at a time. But Filip Rosen left his king where it was, although the danger loomed ever larger now. And this particular game couldn't end in a draw.

The group had held weekly meetings during August, usually chaired by Gunnar or Luffe. Otto kept quiet. He was under strict orders not to do anything on his own. The group seemed to have reverted to a kind of discussion club, which suited the cautious Søren very well—until that September day when Gunnar made his move.

To all outward appearances Gunnar's relationship with Irene was the same as ever. She visited often, although maybe she was a little quieter and more withdrawn than before.

Lars kept out of her way and seldom spoke to her directly, but one day he had met her in the long corridor at school, the one connecting the two sections of the building. She was coming one way, he was going the other, carrying a pile of math books. She was empty-handed. They walked toward each other like two people in a no-man's-land. The distance felt like a mile to him. Outside it was pouring. He had decided to pass her with only a brief nod when she said, "Lars, are we enemies or something?"

He had shifted his pile of books.

"Enemies? No—but . . ."

And at this moment time stopped; even the rain ceased. She glanced away. Then she said, "I—I sometimes cycle out to the old café in the woods, in the afternoon. I don't really know why, but it's so sort of sad and beautiful out there."

She had said those words in August. He knew them by heart.

Five days later, against his better judgment, he found himself cycling out there through the woods. For three-quarters of an hour he wandered restlessly around the café, feeling the desolation of the place for himself. He was both relieved and disappointed.

He hadn't been back.

Now he and Otto were cycling into town and then on to St. Petri. It turned out to be a historic, or anyway a decisive, meeting.

Gunnar nodded at them in a formal way when they came up the stairs. Søren sat by himself, a little apart from the others. A model railroad set was laid out on the long oak table. It included tracks, cars, and buildings both large and small, detailed models of the real thing. Most of it had been made by the owner of the set, Luffe's father, whose hobby began where his work left off.

Only now did Lars see exactly what Luffe had set up on the large table. Everything was perfectly accounted for: the rolling stock depot, the office, the platforms, the station itself, the roadbed, the tunnel. There were locomotives and cars on the rails: freight cars, passenger cars, dining cars. Luffe himself was unusually quiet. Something had been going on before Lars and Otto arrived.

Gunnar took up his chair at the end of the table, with Luffe and Søren on its two long sides and Lars and Otto at the far end. Lars saw that Otto couldn't keep his eyes off the wonderful toy. He looked as though his fingers itched to play with it.

"In a little while," said Gunnar gravely, "in ten minutes or so, Axel Terkelsen is coming up. We need one more man."

This was the strange new Gunnar talking, the Gunnar who no longer joined in conversation with their father and Rosen after dinner. The Gunnar who didn't let Lars know what he was thinking, at least not until his ideas were well formed. This irritated Lars, but there was alarm behind his irritation, an anxiety to which he couldn't put a name. He felt a kind of remorse, although he wasn't sure why. And he was afraid of what all this might lead to.

All the fun and laughter they used to have was a thing of the past.

He had been in Rosen's room one evening recently. Rosen seemed to want to discuss the new organ pipes, but Lars had changed the subject.

"Maybe what the saboteurs are doing isn't really any use," he had said. "In the long run, I mean."

For once Rosen had answered in very concrete terms.

"No doubt you're right, from a military viewpoint. But if it's our hearts, our minds, our integrity we're saving, then no sacrifice is too large or too small . . . not even death."

Lars now looked at Søren, who was inspecting the model railroad with an indulgent little smile, as if to tell the others that for all he cared they were welcome to play with toy trains, so long as no one took it seriously. But a treacherous bead of sweat on his upper lip gave him away. Søren knew what was about to happen.

"Through his father, Luffe's found out about various plans. They're the reason for this model," Gunnar announced.

Søren laughed aloud and looked at Luffe.

"We now know for certain that over the next few weeks we'll have a chance to get some—some of the explosives we need from the big depot here."

Otto looked attentively at Gunnar. Lars cleared his throat and asked what precisely they had in mind.

Gunnar pointed to the depot and had embarked on a long speech when Søren put his hand up, an incredulous expression on his face. Reluctantly, Gunnar crossed his arms over his chest and nodded for him to speak.

"Thanks, Mr. Balstrup, oh, thanks very much indeed," said Søren, with exaggerated politeness. "And thanks a million for being so kind as to inform us rank-and-file members what the rest of you are up to. I take it your great plans are already at an advanced stage?"

"I'm sure you can understand that for reasons of security we—I mean Luffe and I—thought it better to wait until the whole thing was more definite," Gunnar replied.

"Yes, well, of course you might not be able to rely on the rest of us," said Søren with emotion. "Is it brother Lars you don't trust, or our friend Hvidemann here, or is it by any chance me? Could be interesting to know."

"It's you." Gunnar was looking straight at Søren now, and Søren dropped his role of injured innocence.

Lars felt sorry for him. There was no need for this.

Søren asked when he had last let Gunnar down, or any other member of the group.

"Never," said Gunnar. "But then we've never planned to break into a depot and steal explosives before."

"For God's sake, you're not really suggesting that?" whispered Søren. "Gunnar, look at me. You can't be serious! Luffe! What's the matter with you all? The depot! The depot is swarming with soldiers. Men on guard and I don't know what else. We'd simply be mowed down! Are you totally, absolutely out of your minds? And what in heaven's name would we be using these explosives *for?* Tell me that, Gunnar!"

Neither Gunnar nor Luffe answered. They just sat there like stone statues, staring at their model railroad.

"Is it a secret?" inquired Søren. "Aren't the rest of us fit to know any more—Lars and Hvidemann and me? Or am I the only one who's to be kept in the dark?"

"For now," replied Gunnar.

"For now!" yelled Søren. "Just who the hell do you think you are, Gunnar Balstrup! Look, this is my life you're playing with. It's my corpse you're throwing to the Germans! Don't you think you and Luffe ought to put me in the picture?"

"Is it?" Gunnar was looking at his fingers.

"Is it what?"

"Is it your life? Are you with us or aren't you? That's the only question. I don't need to ask Lars, and I certainly don't need to ask Otto Hvidemann."

Søren jumped up and went around the table. "Well, that's obvious. That's damn well obvious, Gunnar," he said angrily. "As for Hvidemann here"—he pointed to Otto's back—"he'd happily set fire to everything in sight and blow their HQ sky-high at the same time if you asked him to. Am I right, Hvidemann?"

Otto glanced at Søren in bewilderment. "Their HQ? You mean the Germans' headquarters?"

"Yes, as a matter of fact I *was* thinking of that. Wouldn't you gladly put three sticks of dynamite under the whole building if Gunnar asked you nicely? Give me an honest answer, Otto."

Otto looked away from Søren and around at the rest of them, seemingly confused by what was going on.

"Well, yes," he said. "Is that what we're about to do?"

Søren slammed his hand down on the table so hard that everything jumped.

"There's your man, Gunnar," he shouted. "Why don't you let the idiot loose with the submachine gun he's grabbed for himself and have him mow down the whole bunch, from the commandant to Suckerfish?"

"Well, why not?" said Gunnar dryly. "Whatever you may say, that's the kind of thing we're here for."

Søren leaned over the table and lowered his voice.

"I'll tell you why not, Gunnar Balstrup. Because the very moment this little worker monkey, this little prole so much as fires a single shot that kills a single Nazi, the Germans will retaliate exactly the way they always do. They'll shoot ten innocent people, and they'll do it in the open street to set an example. And where will we be then, Otto Hvidemann?"

"We're at war," said Otto quietly, with the kind of logic that admits no discussion.

Søren flung himself into his chair, with every sign that he thought it a lost cause. "OK, enjoy yourself, Gunnar," he groaned.

The next moment there was a knock at the door. Luffe rose.

"That will be Axel," said Gunnar. "He's been told some of what we're doing. I'll vouch for him personally; we don't have time for any sort of initiation test. Anyway, we only want him to keep watch."

Small, dark, stocky Axel came in, looking around with awe and gratitude.

"Welcome, Axel!" snapped Søren. "You're at war now, old fellow. Congratulations!"

Axel smiled, rather shyly, and sat down on the edge of a

chair. Gunnar told the others that Axel had promised secrecy, and Axel nodded solemnly. Lars knew him as the fat boy of Gunnar's class. He had finally lost his blubber, but he still suffered from the teasing of the past. Lars did not doubt Axel's word for a moment.

"Well now," said Gunnar, sighing, "will anyone who doesn't want to take part in the group's activities anymore please leave the loft?"

Silence. Lars looked at Søren, who immediately raised an objection.

"You mean you want us just to sit here and agree, without any idea what we're letting ourselves in for?"

"Exactly. And we don't go any farther until you and the others accept that condition. One more thing: That's the last time you ever call Otto Hvidemann a little prole. Is that understood?"

Lars glanced at Gunnar, who had his old aura back. His angel wings radiated a luminous glow.

"I'd like everyone who's with us to put his hand up," he said.

Luffe's, Axel's, and Otto's hands shot up like three rockets.

Lars hesitated, but then said, "OK. I'm with you."

Søren just shook his head.

Gunnar finally lost his temper. "Does that mean yes or no?" he snapped.

"Yes. I'm with you," said Søren at last.

Gunnar nodded to Luffe, who quietly began to explain.

"Our operation's timed for one A.M. the day after tomorrow.

The railroad complex is very closely guarded, but we've taken that into account. Axel and Søren will be posted here and here." Luffe pointed to two locations on the roadbed out on the tracks. "As Gunnar was saying, we plan to break into the depot for explosives. Three of us will go in: Gunnar, Lars, and me. Otto will be stationed there, right outside. We have a submachine gun, a rifle, and a Luger. I'll take the submachine gun. Otto will have the rifle. Gunnar will carry the explosives, and Lars will be armed with the Luger. We have a schedule of the guard changes, and we'll give you the details right before we start. Once we have the stuff, Gunnar and I will bring it back here. The rest of you will go home."

"Are questions allowed?" Søren sounded sarcastic again.

Luffe nodded.

"You honestly believe all the German guards are deaf, dumb, and blind, or maybe lame?"

Luffe chuckled, and Axel laughed out loud but then checked himself.

"We're working on a maneuver to distract them," Gunnar explained evenly.

Lars asked what he meant. Gunnar and Luffe exchanged glances.

"Luffe's made a bomb," Gunnar finally said.

Søren's mouth fell open.

"Only a little one," added Luffe.

Otto looked at him with admiration.

"It will be placed here," said Gunnar, pointing to a group of vehicles on the outskirts of the railroad complex.

"In fact, that'll be the start of the whole operation."

"Forgive me if I seem skeptical," said Søren, "but suppose the unthinkable should happen and the little bomb Professor Luffe has cobbled together fails to go off? Suppose it fizzles out? Then what, Gunnar?"

Gunnar glanced at Luffe.

Lars thought this was in fact a good question.

"It won't fizzle out," said Gunnar.

"The bomb told you so itself, I take it?" inquired Søren. "Or maybe Luffe tried it out in the kitchen at home?"

This amused Luffe mightily. Otto smiled too. It was the first time Lars had seen him smile. The idea of setting off a homemade bomb in the kitchen clearly tickled Otto Hvidemann.

"Obviously a number of things could go wrong," said Gunnar. "We can't provide for every contingency. But we can live with that."

"Or die of it," Lars couldn't help saying. Søren gave him a nod of approval.

"*Inter arma silent leges,*" murmured Gunnar, the Latin scholar. "Laws fall silent among arms."

All was quiet after that. As quiet, thought Lars, as it could be in a loft where six young men had just decided to put their lives on the line. Entirely of their own free will.

Gunnar moved toward the table.

"Our group has six members now," he said, "and we have to stick together through thick and thin. Because if just one person fails, he brings everyone else down with him."

Lars looked at Axel, who had been a full member for all of ten minutes. He was staring at Gunnar with the kind of devotion that hits people who have nothing but hope to cling to.

Søren bit his thumbnail. Otto looked the same as ever.

"Maybe we ought to add that we don't want any unnecessary shooting," said Lars.

Gunnar nodded. "Yes, we do want to emphasize that. This is the first time we've been so well armed, and that means we all bear a great responsibility."

Søren inquired whether Otto had absorbed this lesson properly. Otto gave him a look that left no room for doubt.

"On the other hand," Gunnar went on, "we aren't going in there to get captured; let's be quite clear on that point."

"So you just plug away to your heart's content, Otto," said Søren, looking up at the ceiling.

Gunnar asked whether Søren was happy with the way the jobs had been assigned, or if he'd rather have Otto's place by the depot with one of the guns. "We can swap if you insist."

Søren looked away with an odd little smile. "Why are you doing this to me, Gunnar?" he asked.

"Do you or don't you want to swap with Otto?" Gunnar's voice was cold as ice. "I think I ought to tell you that Luffe and I have spent a good deal of time working out who'd be best doing what. And we came to the conclusion that out of everyone in this group"—Gunnar's voice suddenly broke slightly—"out of everyone in this group it is Otto we rely on most."

There was total silence again. Lars glanced at Otto, who shifted in his chair, embarrassed.

An hour later Lars lay on his bed. In his mind's eye, he saw the now-familiar picture of a boy pulling a shallow rowboat through the water after him, looking for mussels. He heard Gunnar out in the hallway. Gunnar hesitated a moment outside the door. It sounded as if he was having difficulty lighting his pipe.

"Come in, Gunnar," said Lars, before his brother got around to knocking.

What Gunnar had to say was brief enough. "I've been telling Father we ought to get Rosen off to Copenhagen as soon as possible. He can go on to Sweden from there."

Lars sat up on the bed. "Have you discussed it with Rosen himself?"

"Rosen is—well, Rosen!" replied Gunnar, and looked out the window into the garden. "Anyway, it's for his own good."

"We may never see him again," murmured Lars, feeling suddenly empty inside.

"I was thinking of us as well," said Gunnar, with his back to Lars. "Our gestapo friend doesn't come to church just to sing hymns. And as you know, we can't afford unnecessary risks."

He was on his way to the door when Lars said, "I'm—I'm scared to death, Gunnar."

Gunnar nodded heavily. "There's nothing I can say except that you can still pull out of it. In fact, personally I think that—that might be the best thing for you to do."

"How do you mean?"

"We have to think of Mother and Father too," said Gunnar. "If anything were to happen. They only have us. And you know Mother."

"You don't make me feel any better when you talk like that," murmured Lars.

Gunnar opened the door. "Well, think it over," he said.

T W E L V E

The day before what they called Operation V for Victory, Lars decided to go out to the woods for a little shooting practice. Not because he expected to use the gun, just to get acquainted with it. Gunnar had come looking for him in the school yard to ask how he was feeling. Luffe was not at school that day; Søren was hanging around with Axel. It was as if they were all in a play, as if everything was running according to a script with a predetermined beginning, middle, and end. Lars said he was feeling fine. Gunnar clapped him on the back and returned to join Søren and Axel.

After school, Lars biked out to Otto's place and waited half an hour until he got off work. They went into the laundry room of the shanty settlement, and in a matter-of-fact way Otto showed him how to use the Luger.

"Aren't you ever afraid, Otto?" Lars asked cautiously.

Otto held the gun in both hands, his arms straight in front of him. "I'm afraid of not coming home," he said.

In the woods, the shots rang out with a sudden crack, followed by a dull echo. It would have been overdoing things to say he felt happy with the Luger. The report, the recoil, and the snap of it in his brain made him feel quite sick. He thought about the bullet in the chamber, just lying there waiting. The finger on the trigger, the pressure, the release. The fraction of a second between life and death. Maybe there was some German staff sergeant or other sitting in his room right now, looking at his unshaven face, cursing because he has drawn night duty. Maybe his uniform is hanging over his chair, thought Lars. He takes a quick bath and puts the uniform on, enjoying the ritual, all the buttons, the stripes, and so on distinguishing him from the enlisted men. On the table is his belt, with his pistol and its holster. There's a magazine in the pistol, and a bullet in the magazine: a bullet that will find its mark in me.

The rain came suddenly. Lars hadn't intended to go all the way out to the old café, but the shower was so heavy that it would have been silly not to, unless he wanted to catch a cold.

He pedaled hard, remembering his mother bustling about the kitchen as he left home, hearing her sing that popular song: "Comrade, comrade of the sun, friend of the bright blue sky."

He supposed he could have said, "Mother, Gunnar and I are going over to the railroad depot tonight. We're going to steal some explosives. You may never see either of us alive again."

And his mother, removing a half-smoked cigar from her mouth, might have answered casually, "Well, that's how the cookie crumbles, son! Just be sure you two bold Balstrup boys shoot down as many Nazi swine as possible, and I personally will see that the mortician gives you a couple of good solid coffins. Then Rosen can give us a tune on the ivories: 'Light as a bird, a bird in fligh-it; why, oh why, don't we all of us try it?' "

You have to laugh, Lars told himself as he rode through the rain. That's why Rosen has his Chinese silk dressing gown, and why Luffe's always giggling. This war is crazy. You really have to laugh.

Her bicycle was propped in the doorway under the eaves. She was standing inside with her arms wrapped around her, looking very cold. Summer had left the old café. There was a sour autumn odor about its wet wood. He smiled briefly at her.

"What a downpour!" He took his cap off.

She stayed where she was, shifting from foot to foot like a nervous horse. Her hair was dry, which meant she had been there for some time. She looked at him with huge, inquiring eyes, their pupils enlarged.

"Was that you shooting? I heard some shots a little while ago."

They sat down side by side, leaning against the bare wall,

but with a foot or so between them. An air-raid shelter, he thought. Suddenly he had the Luger in his hands. There it lay, as if it were nothing much. Against his will, he relished its aura of heroism and mystery.

"Where on earth did you get that? It's a German pistol, isn't it?"

"Yes, that's right."

She looked away.

"Gunnar thinks I'm blind," she murmured sadly.

Lars put the gun back in his pocket. He was already annoyed with himself for showing it to her. Outside, the rain had stopped. A moment later the sun broke through, very bright. It hung so low in the sky now that its rays struck the café like those from the flaming rocket launcher called a Stalin Organ. She was looking straight into it, her face bathed in a golden, blinding light, totally unreal. Like something in a dream.

"My mother's really sweet," she whispered, as if to herself. "She understands everything. She sees everything. I'll be nineteen at Christmas. This was my only summer to be eighteen. I'll never get it back again. Everything will be different next year. Have you read Kaj Munk? I've kind of come to a halt. All I do is sit in my room, looking out of the window, listening to time passing. Thinking of all we're losing."

"I don't think I know what you mean."

"I mean the Germans! All the things we mustn't do, all the things we *can't* do. And now, of all times, when—when every day's so precious."

"Is it that bad? I mean, there are other countries where—"

"Well, I suppose it isn't really." Her voice rose. "But there's all the rest of it too. I don't know why, but I can't seem to be really happy. Not the way things are now. There's a kind of a veil muffling everything. Always something oppressive weighing us down, as if we were a hundred years old. But I'm not a hundred. I'm eighteen! I'm young! I want to be young; I want to be free and do exactly what I feel like doing."

"Yes, but you—"

"I know perfectly well what you and your friends are up to. Some of it, anyway." She lowered her head so that her chin touched her knees. "So much life," she whispered.

He gazed at her. He could lean a few inches sideways and kiss her ear, her cheek, her soft mouth. He could hold her and tell her . . . tell her all sorts of things.

She looked straight at him. That look, he thought, is like staring into the sun.

Suddenly the glazed double doors were flung open. Lars jumped. They were on their feet as if someone had snapped out an order.

The German noncommissioned officer looked at them without too much surprise. Nor was whatever surprise he did feel unpleasant, judging by his gestures. He had an arrogant expression on his face and a slight twitch at the corners of his mouth. There was an enlisted man behind him. They were both about thirty years old.

The officer strode across the room, turned, and inspected

Lars and Irene, who were standing pressed close to the wall. She had taken Lars's hand. Her hand in mine, he thought. Now all I have to do is take the Luger in my other hand.

"Berger!" called the officer, without taking his eyes off Lars and Irene.

The soldier came in, a knowing smile on his lips. He was half drunk. Lars followed Irene's glance. A little way off, under the trees, stood a German army car. Two girls in light summer dresses were standing in front of it, repairing their makeup. Danish girls, the sort who would sleep with Germans and were known as army mattresses.

The tall noncommissioned officer came slowly over to Lars. He still had a small smile, but his eyes were cold as a fish's. His glance moved on to Irene like the beam of a lighthouse. Crooking his forefinger, he tilted her face up to chuck her gently under the chin.

"Hmmm," he murmured. "Berger, *wo bist du?* Where are you?"

He looked Irene's body up and down and clicked his tongue softly. Then he gave a broad smile and pinched Lars's cheek. He had too many teeth, a smile with far too many teeth. Anatomically incorrect. He looked hard at Lars, almost affectionately. Then his knee came up between Lars's legs, hitting him in the groin. The smile was moving to his eyes now. There was something shiny about them. He smelled of something or other, some kind of disinfectant. With a sudden movement he pulled Irene close to him and kissed her hard. Lars held tight to the Luger in his pocket. He wanted to do it; there was nothing he would rather do. He wanted to empty the magazine, and yet he didn't move. Irene tore herself away from the officer and spit contemptuously on the floor.

"You filthy swine," she said furiously, and marched over to the door.

The officer with the incredible set of teeth put his head back and laughed. Lars hurried after her, edging past the soldier in the doorway.

They cycled back without exchanging a word. She knew I had the Luger in my pocket, he thought. She knew it was loaded, and now she knows I'm too much of a coward to use it.

She stopped at the crossroads just before they reached town. He could see she had been crying.

"I know just what you mean," he said quietly.

"I was—I was going to leave a message for you, on the wall back there," she said.

"For me," he murmured.

She nodded and looked away. "For you. But—well, I won't be going there anymore, not now."

He watched her leave until she turned out of sight.

It was cold at nightfall. Cold and silent. They were crouching there, all of them gazing down at the flat oblong of the railroad complex, where the tracks, the buildings, the platforms, the office, and last but not least the depot were the perfect image of the model Luffe had constructed up in the church loft. Otto and Luffe had their guns ready. There was a feeling in the air that there was no going back. Gunnar sat there with his empty backpack. All he held in his hands was a flashlight.

Axel and Søren had their own small signal flashlights. Gunnar looked at his watch and nodded to them. They disappeared into the dark. Soon it was Luffe's turn. It was twenty to one in the morning. Down on the tracks a couple of guards were marching back and forth.

Now all they had to do was wait.

Ten minutes later, Luffe was back, breathless but cheerful. He nodded to Gunnar. They worked their way silently down the slope and then, crouching low, past the first rails of the tracks. Gunnar knelt down behind an empty freight car. He looked at his watch. Five minutes. Luffe gave Lars a strained smile and crossed his fingers. Their nerves were on edge. The seconds crawled by. Four minutes now.

"I made it with an egg timer," Luffe whispered to Otto, who was staring grimly at the depot. Three minutes to go. Then a group of soldiers, seven in all, jumped down from a truck that stood in the middle of the complex. They were shouting something or other to one another, and they wore big heavy overcoats. Two minutes.

The German soldiers separated, ready to start a long night's guard duty.

"They're a bit late, according to the schedule," murmured Gunnar.

One minute.

Luffe swallowed a lump in his throat. Lars looked down at his boots. If the bomb fizzled out, they could go home again. Steal away as quietly as they had come. Closing his eyes, he saw the picture before him once more. It had haunted him like a nightmare the whole time they'd been waiting. The

German officer in the old café, the man with too many teeth. The smell of some chemical. It struck Lars for the first time that it was the smell of sickness. The man had a smile like a grinning skull.

There was a hollow booming sound over to their left.

Gunnar nodded to Luffe, who raised his fists. Panic broke out; the guards chased back and forth in confusion. Some of them took up positions and stayed put, while others headed down to the freight car from which smoke was rising.

Gunnar said, *"Now!"* and ran across the complex, crouching low, followed by Luffe, Lars, and Otto.

A moment later they were flattening themselves against the wall of the depot. With some difficulty, Luffe got the heavy door open. It was dark inside.

"Ten minutes, Hvidemann," said Gunnar quietly. "If we're not back in ten minutes, you go in."

Otto looked at him apologetically and said he was afraid he didn't have a watch. They gave him Luffe's. "It's waterproof," whispered Luffe cheerfully. The next moment they were inside the depot.

It seemed bigger and gloomier than they had expected from the outside. The freight cars stood waiting like slumbering dinosaurs. Air came in from a ventilator somewhere. Luffe threaded his way through the multitude of cars. Somewhere a dog barked. Gunnar pointed eagerly to the door of one of the cars and produced a crowbar. Luffe stood there with the submachine gun, and Lars took out his Luger. They watched Gunnar struggle with the door. When he began hammering at it, Luffe shook his head. Was that the sound of footsteps?

Gunnar's glance flickered; he yanked on the crowbar for all he was worth. The hinge came off and clattered onto the cement floor. Gunnar just had time to jump up and force himself into the car before a yellow overhead light clicked on. The dog was barking like a creature possessed. Lars and Luffe scrambled into the freight car and helped Gunnar close the heavy door.

Luffe got to work at once. He was investigating stacks of wooden crates when Gunnar said, "The hinge. We forgot the damn hinge and padlock. They're out there on the floor."

Shouted commands echoed in the distance.

"Hell. We can't stay here," said Lars.

Luffe announced that he'd found what they were after and began cramming sticks of dynamite, fuses, primers, and safety catches into Gunnar's backpack.

"That'll do, Luffe," whispered Lars. "That's enough." But Luffe went on and on, like a child let loose in a toy store.

"We'll have to wait in here," said Gunnar. "Damn that hinge and padlock."

Lars took hold of the door. "I'll get them. Then we'll wait till everything quiets down."

Gunnar pushed the door open, and Lars jumped out. The whole depot was awash with yellow light now, so he had no difficulty spotting either the hinge or the padlock. From a dark corner, a dog came racing toward him, a black German shepherd.

Lars felt his feet take root in the ground. The hinge and padlock fell from his hands, hitting the floor with a loud metallic clang. Gunnar called to him. Outside, sirens had begun to howl. The sounds inside the depot intensified. Running feet, the shrill screech of whistles. Doors opening and closing. And the dog barking and snarling as it raced forward. The Luger in his hand, the magazine in the gun, the bullet in the magazine . . .

"Lars!" shouted Gunnar as the shot rang out.

The dog fell over and lay still. Lars had shot it in the head. For a long moment there was no sound. Lars stared speechlessly at the dog, which was stone dead, while Luffe and Gunnar jumped out of the freight car and crouched down to peer between the wheels. More and more lights came on; then there were more voices, more people running.

"Follow me," whispered Gunnar.

They saw the first soldiers through the wheels of the cars. They knew they'd have to go the long way around to get anywhere near the depot door.

"*Halt!*" The guard was standing not far off, aiming his submachine gun at them.

"Run for it!" shouted Gunnar.

They wriggled their way under the cars and out the other side, while the bullets cracked against metal and the air over their heads was thick with fragments. The Germans had opened fire from several directions.

Gunnar flung himself flat on his stomach. Lars covered his ears with his hands.

"Hell! We're going the wrong way," shouted Luffe.

"There *isn't* any other way," replied Gunnar.

The scream of the siren outside cut right through them. They'll come down on us now, thought Lars, the whole damn lot of them will come down on us now.

They stopped for a moment to get their breath back, feeling as if they were playing a game of cat and mouse in this great labyrinth. It was only a question of time.

"We'll have to shoot our way out," Gunnar said grimly. "Are you ready to do that?"

Luffe nodded, but he was staring unhappily into space. Gunnar asked Lars for the Luger; Lars was only too glad to hand it over. At that moment shots whizzed by barely a foot above their heads. Splinters of wood exploded like firecrackers. The boys flung themselves flat again. Lars saw Luffe wriggling his way under a broad coal car as a German guard less than twenty feet away knelt down and took aim. He couldn't possibly avoid hitting poor Luffe, who could only lie and wait for the bullet that would end his life. But now the sound of shots splitting the air came from quite a different direction. The boys stared at the soldier, who, after a brief frenzied jerk, collapsed. Like frantic lizards, the group writhed and wriggled to the other side of the cars and into another aisle, where they saw Otto standing with his back to them, firing away for dear life. His aim was deadly.

"Otto!" shouted Gunnar.

"Go on!" Otto shouted back. "I'll keep you covered. Axel and Søren are here too. The Germans are going crazy outside."

"We have to get out, Gunnar," whispered Lars, grabbing his brother.

A hail of bullets smashed through a huge window, sending

glass crashing everywhere in tiny fragments. They stopped, staring speechlessly at the figure kneeling on the floor, shouting and screaming as he flailed about helplessly among the crystal shards. Søren. Axel came running up, shock written all over his face.

"OK," said Gunnar. "Stick close together now. We'll get out yet. I promise you we will."

There was a moment's silence while the Germans took up new positions.

"They must have closed the door by now," said Luffe.

Axel confirmed that they had.

"Otto," said Gunnar. "Can you take Søren? I don't know if he's been hit or not. The rest of us will go down below and see if we can find a back door."

Otto nodded and glanced at Søren, who was still lying under the gaping hole that had once held fifty little windowpanes.

The shouting and screaming began again. Otto ran over and got a firm grip on Søren.

"Come on, Lars," shouted Gunnar. "Run for it—now!"

Søren got to his feet, shaking, and stared at Otto.

"This is all your fault," he hissed. "Your fault, Hvide-mann."

Suddenly a German loomed on the scaffolding above them.

"Otto," called Lars, running back.

He saw Otto whip around and open fire in one and the same movement. The guard dropped with a scream. Søren looked like a sleepwalker as Otto grabbed him by the neck of his shirt. They ran after the others, who had found a narrow metal door at the very back of the building. A flight of stone steps led down to a low-ceilinged, dimly lit corridor. The corridor wound around, right and then left. Gunnar went first, followed by the rest. Outside, the sirens wailed with renewed force.

They entered some kind of storeroom or workshop.

"We're trapped," gasped Axel. "We'll never get out of here, Gunnar. I was going—going to start college next year." He made this last remark in a low, incredulous voice.

"Of course we'll get out," snapped Gunnar. "The only question is whether *you'll* get accepted to college."

Søren had collapsed on a pile of sacks. The whites of his eyes shone with a fear such as Lars had never seen before. Meanwhile, the others were looking for an exit.

"Buried alive," muttered Søren. "I said so, didn't I? I told you so, but you wouldn't listen. . . ."

Gunnar was shushing him when a locker door slowly swung open. This gradual, apparently accidental movement immediately attracted Lars's attention. The soldier was about his own age and appeared to have been hiding behind the door. His jacket was unbuttoned, and he was unarmed. Just like me, thought Lars.

"Gunnar," he called. "Gunnar, we have a problem here."

There was silence. Gunnar and Luffe stared at the soldier, who was whispering something. *"Bitte . . . bitte . . . bitte . . ."* "Please," he was saying. "Please."

They formed a circle around him. Søren was screaming in pain.

"What do we do with this German?" asked Lars.

"He'll know us again," cautioned Luffe. "And that'll finish us."

Gunnar rubbed his face; he looked angrily at Søren, who had flung himself down on the floor. Otto made his way over to the German and, with a determined expression, began loading his rifle. Lars quickly intervened.

"Otto, you can't just shoot him, for God's sake!" he gasped. "Gunnar, say something!"

"But he'll kn-kn-know us again," repeated Luffe. "He can identify us."

Gunnar and Otto exchanged glances. Otto flung open the metal door of the locker, forced the German back into the narrow space behind it, and bolted it shut.

Axel came rushing up. "Here—over here. A window! A window!"

It was round and not very big, but they clambered through it one by one. They found themselves on the right-hand side of the railroad tracks. The siren was still wailing, and searchlights were still sweeping the area.

Gunnar ran for it, crouching low. Luffe and the others followed him, with Otto and Lars bringing up the rear.

Bullets peppered the tracks.

"Run," shouted Gunnar. "Don't turn around, just run as fast as you can. It's only a hundred yards."

Three Germans calmly knelt down and took aim.

Lars saw Otto stop.

"No, Otto, for God's sake—come on, man!"

Otto fired. Then he was running after Lars again. A final

shot tore through the night. Lars turned and saw Otto fall briefly to his knees before toppling forward.

The icy blue beam of a searchlight fixed its cold eye on the body lying there. Lars shouted. Gunnar called back to Lars, crying that it was now or never. But Lars ran back and dragged Otto halfway to his feet. Otto stared at Lars with a feverish expression on his face. Then Gunnar and Luffe came back too. Between them, they got Otto over to the slope, where Axel was waiting with the backpack.

As they struggled up the slope, Lars saw that Otto's shoulder was soaked with blood.

Søren brought the bicycles over. Axel said he'd wet his pants.

"Yes, OK," panted Gunnar. "Søren and Axel, you get moving. Now! Go on!"

Luffe put Otto down on the ground. Otto asked for a glass of water; he was completely dazed. Lars tried to apply a tourniquet.

"We can't take him to a hospital," Gunnar said when Axel and Søren were gone. "The police would be called."

"So what?" snapped Lars. "He'll bleed to death here."

Luffe nodded. "He has to see a doctor, Gunnar. Quickly too."

Lars caught hold of Gunnar. "Kirsten's father has his own consulting room. It's not so far away. If we can prop Otto up on a bike . . ."

"But it's the middle of the night," objected Gunnar.

"Who the hell cares!" Lars retorted. They balanced Otto on Gunnar's bicycle, so that Gunnar could hold him and steer at the same time. Luffe placed a hand on the seat and pushed.

"Away we go, Hvidemann," said Gunnar. "Do your best not to fall off."

Fifteen minutes later they arrived. By now Otto was unconscious. Luffe and Lars laid him down on the grass outside the big brick house while Gunnar rang the doorbell.

A moment passed; then a light came on. The doctor himself opened the door, in his pajamas and bathrobe. Gunnar apologized for disturbing him so late and explained that a friend was in urgent need of help.

They carried Otto into the consulting room, where the doctor took a quick, searching look at his shoulder.

"How did this happen?" he asked sharply.

"I can't tell you that," Gunnar answered.

The doctor looked from one to another of them. His eyes came to rest on Lars.

"Now then, what's going on here?" he asked crossly. "Just what are you boys up to?"

"Excuse me, but he has a bullet in his shoulder, Dr. Halling," said Lars politely.

"Yes, I can see that. I can also see that this boy works at the Kolstrup Brickyard."

Otto was indeed wearing his overalls with the brickyard's initials on them.

"He's not one of my patients."

"What the hell does that mean?" asked Gunnar.

"I mean exactly what I say."

"But—but your Hippocratic oath!" exclaimed Gunnar, staggered. "You can't refuse to—"

The doctor took a couple of steps toward the door.

"Out!" he said. "Just get out! The emergency room is open all night. Do you think I'm going to help a bunch of young hooligans? As for you two, Lars and Gunnar, I wouldn't have thought it of you. Kindly remove this working-class scum from my consulting room, or I'll—"

The doctor stopped short, staring into the muzzle of Gunnar's Luger.

"Get started, please."

"Not on your life." The stout little man crossed his arms and took a step forward.

"I personally," said Gunnar, "have shot ten Germans tonight. So one more isn't going to make much difference. In fact, I think it would be a real pleasure to free the country of another Nazi sympathizer."

"What the devil do you think you're doing, you little puppy?" shouted the doctor.

Here Gunnar lost his temper. The next moment he had taken the doctor by the scruff of his neck and was almost ramming the barrel of the pistol up his nostrils.

Lars gasped.

"I promise you, Dr. Halling," said Gunnar, "if you don't help this boy, I'll shoot you."

It took just under half an hour to patch Otto up. He was still feeling rather weak as the doctor, washing his hands in the sink, informed them that the Wehrmacht would eventually even things up with Otto.

"If you so much as utter a word about all this," said Gunnar, "you're a dead man."

On the way back, Luffe suggested that Otto could use a beer after losing all that blood. Otto said that was no problem.

A little later they were sitting with their backs to the brewery wall, drinking straight from a pail. Luffe's words were already slurred when he asked, "How come you know your way around here so well, Otto?"

"My father worked in the brewery for twelve years," said Otto, taking Lars's hand to help him up on his feet.

A smile passed between them as they each grabbed a blue porcelain handle. The wail of the sirens sounded raucously over the town.

Gunnar and Luffe shook hands. Lars was about to give Otto a bear hug when he remembered the wounded shoulder. So he pounded him on the other arm instead.

·

THIRTEEN

Søren asked Gunnar for a private meeting—just the two
of them. Gunnar replied that, as had been agreed, they were
taking a break in their operations. "But the Germans aren't,"
shouted Søren right across the big school hall. Gunnar stared
at him. Søren laughed hysterically. "Things are getting out
of control," he said. "Out of your control anyway, old man!"

Just under a week had passed. The group had already tried
to get things into perspective and decided on a rest. Lars had
confided in Axel, who was the sort of person you quickly
came to trust. There was something basically dependable
about the quiet boy who had gone straight into the line of fire
without a murmur—and most important of all, without boast-
ing of it later.

"You know, I sometimes put my head under the quilt in

the afternoon and dream I'm not here," Lars told him on the way home from school. "I pretend the war's over, the soldiers have gone home, and Hitler's back with his paintbrushes in Austria. Or maybe they've fined him or sent him to jail. I avoid thinking about the depot. I try to forget Søren lying in all that broken glass. . . . Well, I try to forget the whole thing, in fact."

Axel nodded and adjusted his tie. He said he felt something similar, only kind of the other way around. "I've never been—how can I put it—so tensed up, so *fulfilled*. The whole thing was so overpowering. It was fantastic."

Lars nodded wisely. "It's a substance that works on the body like a drug."

"A drug?"

"You can get hooked on it, for a while anyway. But that doesn't last. It passes, or maybe common sense eats it up—big, strong white blood corpuscles or something—until finally, well, you're just scared. Afraid the whole thing is about to begin again, and history will repeat itself, but this time your luck will change and the grinning skull will catch up with you."

Lars stared off into space. Axel glanced at him anxiously, walked with him a little while longer, and then left. Lars watched him go. Just as well. It was a good idea to be alone; he needed to be by himself, find somewhere quiet, a place where the wind blew as usual and September was just September, a dry, beautiful month, a listening kind of month. He needed to let the fresh, strong wind blow the earth clean, and forget. But in dreams, when sleep overtook him, every-

thing came back, more absurd than ever, as though his unconscious was determined to create system and order out of
the madhouse of reality.

In his dream . . . in his dream, he is running and running,
falling, getting up, stepping on broken glass. He must and
will reach the black iron door. The handle—quick, Lars,
quick. Get it open. Finally he does, and stares at the smiling
German officer motioning him in. A hospitable man. His
mouth is like a great gash in his pale face. Something's
happening to him. His skin is stretching, melting as if it were
too close to a fire. His hair curls like ashes. His eyes are
separate from the rest of his face. His uniform's burning,
everything is burning, until finally there's nothing left but his
smile and his laughter. Run, Lars, run . . .

He opens the door and goes into the old café. The place
is bathed in yellow light. "Is there anyone here?" Irene calls.
Her voice comes from somewhere else. He turns, and there
she is. Her lips, her kiss, at last. "I've left you a message."
She smells of something or other. Disinfectant. Lars tries to
free himself, but she holds tight. Her arms are strong. Her
soft lips curl back so that he can see her endless set of teeth.
He moves in the round arena of the old café like a horseback
rider in a dressage display. The swastika is painted on the
walls, people are clapping, the flag is hoisted, and at the
very back, among the spectators, sits Filip Rosen in a prison
uniform. He has no hair. His cheeks are hollow. Lars is
caught in the searchlight's icy blue beam.

The people have risen to their feet. They're singing.

"Outside the barracks, by the colored light
I'll always stand and wait for you at night.
We will create a world for two
I'll wait for you the whole night through."

Lars puts his uniform on. It fits perfectly: cap, boots, and belt. Kirsten has flowers in her hair. She looks like a Tyrolean girl. She curtsies to him. They are wearing wedding rings, and her braided hair lies like golden ropes on her neck. Her plump, determined neck.

"I'll wait for you the whole night through,
For you, Lili Marlene; for you, Lili Marlene."

He woke up, bathed in sweat, to find Gunnar standing there in his old bathrobe. Gunnar smiled and was about to lay a hand on Lars's fevered forehead, but Lars drew back.
"Be careful, Gunnar."
"You're dreaming, Lars."
"No, be careful."
"Careful of what?"
"Careful of me."
"It's OK, I'll look after you."
"That wasn't what I meant."

All the boys at school were summoned into the main hall, where the principal and some of the teachers, including the ever-zealous Junkersen, had them line up in rows.

This was just a routine visit by the Wehrmacht, the principal told them. Three Germans—two enlisted men and an officer—and the man the boys called Suckerfish entered from the school yard. Junkersen bowed in an obsequious way, while Lars stared at the anemic-looking gestapo man and the thin little soldier he was pushing into the room ahead of him. It was the German soldier from the basement.

"This needn't take much of your time, gentlemen," said Suckerfish as he began at one end of the hall.

Lars stole a look at Luffe and Gunnar, who were both staring into space. Maybe Otto had been right after all, and they should have shot the soldier. Silenced him for good. The little procession stopped in front of Axel, who was sweating profusely. Suckerfish took his time. They moved on down the row toward Lars. They passed Søren, they passed Luffe, and they stopped in front of Gunnar.

The gestapo man walked around Gunnar and stood there behind his back for a while, until the soldier shook his head and went on. Now they were only a short distance from Lars, who caught the eye of his enemy. His enemy, a boy the same age as himself. However, it was not a hostile glance he met; it was the glance of a fellow conspirator. The soldier shook his head and moved on, down the next row. Lars looked at the floor. Someday, he thought, when this nightmare is over, we'll be able to clasp hands, he and I.

The whole thing lasted only a few minutes. In the doorway, Suckerfish turned back to the assembled boys.

"I'm staying here in the town," he said, "until we've caught whoever it was who attacked Wehrmacht troops without provocation, ignoring the wishes of both Danes and Germans. As you know, saboteurs are always captured—or shot."

The gestapo man's remarks hung in the hall. He relished the boys' deference and the alarm he was spreading, and he let an agonizing amount of time drag by.

"If any of you . . . one or more of you . . . feel you want to tell me anything, well, you know where to find me. It would make everything so much simpler—"

"Is that all, sir?" interrupted the principal in a voice that shook. Suckerfish looked at the boys again, nodded, and left.

Gunnar and Luffe exchanged glances.

"Thank you, boys," said the principal. "You may go now."

Later that afternoon, Gunnar and Søren met in the church itself. Lars and Luffe were sitting at the back of the nave. Søren began by saying he wanted to talk to Gunnar alone, but Gunnar insisted that he would be the one to set the conditions. Søren's voice rose.

"We're finished, Gunnar Balstrup, you and me," he said.

Gunnar nodded calmly.

"Oh, yes, you may nod, Gunnar," shouted Søren, "you may well nod. You're in a very strong position right now, very strong. But do you realize you have a murderer in your group? A murderer!" cried Søren in a voice that echoed through the church.

"Søren," asked Gunnar quietly, "where do we draw the line between what you call murderers and what the rest of Denmark calls patriots?"

Søren moistened his lips. "Ever since that Otto Hvide-mann—"

Gunnar interrupted him. "I rather think 'that Otto Hvi-demann' saved your life a few days ago."

"Well, nobody asked him to!" shouted Søren. "But maybe you think I ought to be grateful, is that it? Am I supposed to go out to the shanty settlement and thank him?"

"Staying away from us will be quite enough," observed Gunnar calmly.

Søren backed toward the door, staring at Gunnar, who was standing by the font with one hand in his pocket.

"I just want you to know, Gunnar Balstrup, I just want you to know—here in God's house, I want everyone to know that in the future, in the years to come, I have no intention of lifting a finger for characters like Otto Hvidemann. There seems to be something you've forgotten, Gunnar."

"What's that?"

"Just who we are," cried Søren. "I feel ashamed to look at you."

Søren took a couple of steps toward Gunnar. He was on the verge of tears.

"When I think how the two of us founded the group last year. Remember the things we swore, about decent conduct and pride and honor?"

Gunnar sighed heavily.

"What happened to all that, Gunnar? This is such a mess. But there'll come a day, you mark my words, when the war will be over and people will have to account for themselves.

Then we'll see where we stand. Do you sleep well at night, Gunnar?"

"Go back to your friends in the Young Conservatives," said Gunnar. "You certainly won't be running any kind of risk there. But before you go . . ."

He walked rapidly over to Søren, who glanced around at Lars and Luffe. They had stationed themselves in front of the door.

"Before you go, we need your promise."

"My promise?" Søren blew his nose.

"Yes. You must swear you'll say nothing."

"Look, what do you take me for? What sort of person do you think I am?"

Gunnar put a hand on Søren's shoulder.

"We don't have to be enemies, Søren," he said. "I know I can always rely on you."

Søren looked down at the floor.

"Where's this going to end?" he asked. "Where will it all end, Gunnar?"

Gunnar took him by the shoulders and led him over to the big double doors.

"It will end with the return of freedom," said Gunnar. "That's where it will end."

Søren looked from Gunnar to Lars, and then back at Luffe.

"Good luck, Søren," said Luffe in friendly tones, raising his hand.

Søren took a deep breath.

"OK," he whispered, "OK, but . . . but take care of yourselves."

Lars watched him go.

Luffe shook his head and muttered something about homework to do. Gunnar waited until he had gone, and then produced a note from his inside pocket.

Examining it, Lars recognized their father's handwriting. It said, *For Gunnar,* and there were a couple of typewritten lines on the other side: *Svend Hansen is coming to visit the rectory and the church in the near future.*

Lars looked at Gunnar. "Is this some kind of code?"

"It's an anonymous tip," said Gunnar. "I imagine it has to do with Rosen."

Lars looked at the paper again.

"So who's Svend Hansen?" he asked.

"Suckerfish," murmured Gunnar, crumpling up the note.

At the end of the month the Germans came and turned Rosen's little room upside down. They rummaged around in his private papers, they looked inside his books, and finally, tucked into a biography of Bach, they found a yellow Jewish star.

"Do you know when Mr. Rosen is coming home?" Svend Hansen, otherwise known as Suckerfish, asked Reverend Balstrup. Lars and Gunnar were in the dining room with their mother.

"I think he's away until the day after tomorrow," replied the minister shortly.

"And you have no idea what he's doing? Or where he's gone?"

"Has our organist broken the law?" inquired the minister.

The gestapo man looked around the room. Perhaps by chance, his eyes came to rest on Lars and Gunnar.

"We want to talk to him about the burglary in the railroad depot, among other things," said Suckerfish quietly.

"Rosen?" exclaimed the minister incredulously. "Burglary?"

"Yes, you learn something surprising every day," said the gestapo man, nodding to the minister's wife as he and his men left.

In fact, Rosen was out at a farmhouse, surrounded by five children and two dogs, waiting to hear what had happened. The minister and Gunnar went out there to see him; they returned three hours later, and Gunnar went straight to his room.

"He's going to Copenhagen on Tuesday," the minister told his wife and Lars, who were in the hall.

Mrs. Balstrup was crying. "This is what comes of their sabotage!" she said. "Poor little Rosen."

The minister shook his head sadly, but Lars followed his mother into the kitchen.

"That's wrong," he said firmly.

"What's wrong? Lars, I'm busy. There's a parish council meeting tomorrow."

"What you said is wrong. I really want you to understand that. Please do, Mother."

"What are you talking about, dear?"

"It's not the—the saboteurs' fault the gestapo are looking for Rosen."

"Oh, it isn't?"

"No, it's not! They're just using that as an excuse. So as to turn ordinary people against both the Jews *and* the saboteurs. And I can't bear to see you falling for their propaganda too."

"All I know is we're losing Rosen." She gave Lars a hug and kissed him on the forehead. Lars told himself that of course there was nothing really the matter with her powers of judgment—if these methods worked in the huge country of Germany, then why wouldn't they work in Denmark too?

"I hate them," whispered Lars into her hair.

"Yes," she said, drying her eyes. "To hell with them all!"

They smiled at each other.

F O U R T E E N

He looked out the back window of the bus for a long time, watching the town slowly shrink and become the familiar postcard of itself, with the church in the center. It was just under six miles to the ferry.

Gunnar, his father, and Rosen were sitting in front of him, in their best clothes. They reminded Lars of three morticians, or a trio of deeply serious comedians in some French play set in Montmartre. Suppose Gunnar serves in the funeral home every day, he thought, and the minister and the organist drive the elegant hearse pulled by six black horses. The funeral home is next to Madame Rose's brothel, and in the middle of the night the customers sometimes get the doors mixed up, so then the morticians show themselves in their true colors, and the whole thing turns on Gunnar's love for one of the streetwalkers, plus the revelation that his mother is really Madame Rose, and the funeral home and the brothel are in business together.

Yes, well, you could look at things like that: keep them at a distance in order to go on living with them. Lars decided he preferred his French farce to what they were now doing. He stared at the back of the organist's neck, where the little curls of dark hair needed trimming. Rosen was never untidy, just slightly unkempt. His right hand lay on the armrest. Long slim fingers, fingers with music in them. Notes trickling out, high and low, sending shivers down the congregation's spines.

Father had once said, "I've always dreamed of preaching in a tall, narrow cathedral. I love the Church of Denmark, but I'd like to stand in a Gothic cathedral just once, with its tall spire pointing to heaven. Yes, I wouldn't mind a cathedral."

"We'll build you one, Balstrup," Rosen had said. "It'll be ready next Sunday."

And the next Sunday, Rosen played a prelude he had composed. It transformed the church, lifting the roof and drilling its way right into heaven itself, so that the minister hardly dared enter the pulpit.

Their farewells at home had been almost grotesque. Instead of crying, Mrs. Balstrup had been feverish and excited, all fluttery and talkative.

"Well, well, look who's off to Sweden, where there aren't any air-raid warnings or German soldiers!" she had gushed. As if Rosen were going for a two-week vacation.

Rosen had been the same as ever. He just nodded and

looked quietly around the room. The room that had been his home for so many years. It was easy to read the expression in his eyes: He would never see that room again. He looked at the furniture—the tall grandfather clock, the chest of drawers, the desk, and the pretty pictures—as if he wanted to impress it all on his memory this one last time. When he turned around, a light had gone out. A quiet life had been packed up, put away, the door shut and locked. Father had found a new organist, who was going to begin at once.

Mother hadn't spared Rosen the usual empty phrases about writing often. He suddenly took three dance steps, there in the hallway.

They stared at him, their jaws dropping.

"Why, I've suddenly become a person of importance!" explained Rosen.

"You always were," said Gunnar quietly.

Now the organist turned in the bus seat and looked at Lars.

"Copenhagen's a fine city," he said. "May I see your hand, young man?"

Lars smiled and offered it. The organist studied it gravely.

"Yes, well, that goes without saying." Rosen closed the hand, then turned it over and clenched it firmly as he ran his index finger over the hard knuckles. "And that," he said quietly, "is the other side of life."

Lars could see the little ferry approaching. It gave two small hoots.

They stood on the dock. The minister and Rosen shook hands—shook all four hands very thoroughly and for a long time.

"Well, what must be, must be," murmured the minister.

Gunnar was quiet. To Lars, he seemed like a little boy again, little Gunnar who felt it was his fault if it rained on his birthday.

Gunnar hugged Rosen, who was a head shorter than he was.

"To think I could once pick you up in my arms!" said Rosen.

"Look after yourself, and come back soon." Gunnar stood next to his father, hands crossed in front of him.

They were so like each other, father and son. The organist turned to Lars.

"Well, now I have some thinking about life to do." He smiled. "One ought to think about life now and then, and maybe—maybe I've always been a little afraid of it. Church music doesn't have a great deal to do with reality."

Lars shrugged his shoulders helplessly. There was so much he wanted to say.

"And maybe it's cowardly only to love by mail." Rosen looked out across the water. "But now I'm a refugee, Lars, and you have to stay here. It's your country and your fight."

"It's your country too," said Lars.

"Oh, no—my country's China, and my kind of China is to be found only up here." He pointed to his forehead. "But life, Lars"—Rosen looked gravely at him—"life is worth fighting for."

Lars nodded.

Soon after that, Filip Rosen was on board the ferry and it was setting out again, hooting. The bus headed back to town.

Mother had set the table for coffee. They sat in the dining room, where they could hear the grandfather clock routinely slicing the hours up into little bits. The minister cleared his throat, and Mother said something about a new film. Gunnar said nothing, and a little later Lars went off to his room. He opened the door as they were beginning to discuss the apple crop.

"Good-bye, Rosen," whispered Lars, looking out into the garden, where the October mist hung in the bushes. "And farewell, Nina."

It was nearly four-thirty. The noise of the German brass band grew louder and louder. Swelling, crescendoing, filtering in through every crevice. German boots marching down Østergade as if that were the most natural thing in the world. Out at sea, Filip Rosen would be sitting with his little brown suitcase on his lap. He had left a gaping black hole, a dreadful sense of loss, behind him.

F I F T E E N

They were sitting up at the top of the dimly lit brewery, drinking from shining metal pails of foaming beer. Lars felt a humming in his arms and a buzzing in his head. He glanced at the rifle lying between them. It looked different now that Otto had fit on its telescopic sight. The gun had lost its honest nature. There it was, stealthy, shady, and above all dangerous.

"Always seems to be a gun between us, Otto," he murmured lazily.

Otto cast him a quick glance.

I'm a bit tipsy, thought Lars. Tipsy and foolish. I hope Rosen's a bit tipsy too. Maybe he's dancing, there in Copenhagen; maybe he's with people who think like him, and they're holding hands in a merry dance, laughing through their tears and grief and bitterness. Just as long as he doesn't do anything silly.

Was Otto Hvidemann tipsy too, or stone-cold sober?

That was a phase of getting tipsy, Lars thought, a cynical, naked kind of sobriety, when you faced yourself as you really were. He saw himself as a hesitant, gnomelike little creature, searching out sacred springs under cover of darkness, certain springs in the preserves of night. Drinking from them, lapping them up in secret. He cast quick glances around him in the school yard, in the main street, even in the rectory. His life had suddenly been fit with a telescopic sight. Once he had been cheerful, happy, full of back talk. Always ready with some piece of repartee when he happened to run into her. Now he ran away like a wounded animal when she turned up. Furtive and dishonest, that was the way to describe it.

"Your father, Otto," he managed to say. "What did he die of?"

Otto put his pail down and dried his mouth on his sleeve. "What did he die of?"

"Yes—was he sick?"

"No, he was shot."

It was fall outside, the season in its typical minor key. The musical score was written in the sky. Lars felt the cold touch of sobriety, along with a small, helpless sense of genuine loneliness.

"He was in Spain," said Otto quietly. "Fighting Franco."

Lars nodded as if he understood, although he understood nothing at all.

Unreality, he thought. You don't need to intrude on unreality with information like that. A man goes away from Denmark, leaving his wife and children, travels thousands of miles to a foreign land to fight side by side with people who think as he does, shoulder to shoulder with his comrades. Well, it's in the history books, but as time passes, and less and less gets written about it, it will be gone one day just like Otto's father. The point of it, historically, is that Franco won.

"Your father was killed in the Spanish Civil War," muttered Lars to himself.

"We had a letter the day my little sister was born." Otto's eyes became distant. "It was written in Spanish. We didn't know Spanish, and we didn't know anyone who did. But the midwife knew a lady who knew Latin. So we all took the bus out to see her. My mother sat on the lady's green sofa, holding the baby. The rest of us stood by the wall. We knew the letter must be from my father or someone who knew him. We hadn't heard anything from him in six months. The lady out there in the country couldn't actually translate the letter, but she could tell that my father was dead. She said, 'I think anyone could read and understand that news in any language, Mrs. Hvidemann.' "

Lars closed his eyes and leaned his head back.

"Then what, Otto?" he asked quietly.

"Then we caught the bus home again."

Lars looked straight at him.

"You're my best friend," Lars said.

Otto glanced at him, surprised. Lars nodded. A long moment passed, almost too long a moment, and then Otto's rare smile broke out, showing through his dark gaze like the sun briefly, momentarily, breaking through the clouds. You felt thankful for it.

"I'd be very proud if . . . ," Lars heard himself begin. Otto looked at his hands. Lars murmured something about Filip Rosen, but for some reason that didn't seem to interest Otto. Finally there was just silence. The brewery had its own noises, but Lars felt cut off, shut away in this new, impenetrable solitude.

"Otto," he said, "have you ever been in love?"

Otto stared at him, baffled, but then smiled broadly as if Lars had said something rather sexy.

"With a girl?"

"Yes, with a girl," sighed Lars, thinking it was useless to keep bringing his own world to the notice of this poor boy who seemed to have been born on a different planet.

"I think I was, once."

Lars stared at him. How did Otto always manage to pull the rug out from under you?

"Really, Otto? I mean . . . in love?"

Otto thought it over for a while. "With my cousin. We were at the cattle show. It lasted half an hour."

Lars moved over to Otto and put an arm around his shoulders. "A person isn't in love just for half an hour, you dummy."

"Well, I was."

Lars let go of him. "OK, what happened?"

"Nothing. She wanted to kiss, and I didn't."

Lars nodded, and wondered why he always started nodding

when he didn't understand something he had just been told.

"I'm in love," he said baldly.

Otto picked the rifle up.

"Are you listening, Otto Hvidemann? I'm in love. This minute, the whole time, all around the clock. I feel her burning inside me."

Otto looked through the telescopic sight.

"And I don't know which way is up. My head's in a whirl. I think of her all the time. This is a secret, of course."

"Do you want to shoot her?"

Lars felt as if he were emerging from a deep well. Down in the well, he had heard Otto ask, Do you want to shoot her? So what was he doing down in the well, anyway? Hiding, of course.

"Shoot her? Look, are you totally nuts, Hvidemann?" Oh, yes, of course, I could always shoot her, he thought. And myself as well. "I'm in love with her, and you don't shoot the person you love, Otto."

"You know where that cognac comes from?"

Lars waved his arms about. "Why can't you talk like everyone else, Otto?" He sounded almost angry. "Can't you talk to me normally, just this once? Can't you answer me without suddenly saying such ridiculous things? *What* cognac?"

"That cognac back at our place."

Lars waited. Otto was looking at him with a peculiar smile. Not a happy smile.

"OK, tell me where it comes from," sighed Lars, without much interest.

Otto rose to his feet.

"Come on," he said. "We're going out."

Lars reminded him that they couldn't go around town with a rifle.

"We'll keep to the shadows," whispered Otto. He did not seem to be quite himself.

The house was large, white, and very handsome—a grand villa in the best part of town. At least twenty cars were parked outside the broad flight of stairs at the front. Danish as well as German cars. The guard at the door lit a cigarette. There was a faint sound of dance music.

Otto seemed quite at home as he circled around the back-yard, where there was an annex with a flat roof. He picked up a ladder from the ground. Lars joined him.

"What the hell are we doing here?" he whispered, shaking himself.

Otto pointed. Inside the villa they could see a large party in progress. German soldiers, or, rather, German officers. Men in black gestapo uniforms and pretty women in party dresses. They were enjoying themselves, talking, dancing, drinking.

"Army mattresses," murmured Lars, and saw Otto looking through the telescopic sight.

"I think we'd better clear out of here, Otto."

"Want to look?" Otto handed him the rifle without taking his eyes off the villa.

"My God!" exclaimed Lars, staring through the telescopic sight. The party had suddenly come quite close. He could almost smell it. Bottles and glasses: vermouth, whiskey, gin, cognac. An officer with lipstick on his cheek, a pretty woman's earlobe. A gold tooth in a mouth thrown back in soundless laughter, a pearl necklace draping a low-cut neckline, a hairy wart on a man's fat neck. Foreheads, cheeks, eyes, calves, knees, fingers, tongues, nostrils, uniforms, Nazi badges. A black-clad arm slipped around a slender waist in the dance. A peremptory gesture, a quick kiss dropped on the woman's neck. She laughed and spun around, smiled and slipped back into the man's embrace. Otto's mother.

Lars lowered the rifle, staring straight ahead. The party was a comfortable distance away again. Its sounds seemed to be returning: laughter and music. Lars had just surfaced. Down there in the deep water he had seen something he ought not to have seen. Something he'd rather forget. Another secret.

"Let's go, Otto," he said.

"This is where we get our booze," muttered Otto, and raised the rifle against his cheek.

"For God's sake, Otto! It's not worth it! Can't you just for once listen to what I say?"

The shot crashed through the night, shattering the window. Angular pieces of glass twirled in the yellow light. There was a loud squeal from the gramophone, and some shouting. A shrill whistle ran from house to garden like a line linking them. Panic.

Lars ran after Otto, who moved like a cat through the alleys, gateways, and dark narrow streets of the night-empty town.

They stood in the shadows of the marketplace, gasping for breath. Otto's glance flickered. Lars tried to find the right words. He wanted to say: Don't take it so hard, Otto, for goodness' sake, your mother's still young and pretty, and I expect she'd like a little luxury in her life.

Instead, he said, "It's Irene I'm in love with. Gunnar's girlfriend. It's a secret—it's a disaster too."

Despite everything, this seemed to bring Otto down to earth. He looked at Lars as if he were merely registering the facts, and soon after that he was gone. Lars saw him disappear like a ghost.

Lars lay in bed. I told Otto, he thought. I confided in him. But he wasn't really interested in either Irene or Rosen.

He turned on his side, and only then did he find the note under his pillow. It was very short. *Suckerfish has been here. G.*

S I X T E E N

He stood outside his brother's door a moment, listening. Then he knocked. It was a few minutes past midnight. Lars pushed the door open and saw Gunnar sitting at his desk. A handwritten letter, a fountain pen, and a corncob pipe lay in front of him.

"Come in." His voice sounded tired but welcoming.

Lars sat down in the heavy armchair in the corner. The chair where Gunnar was going to sit and study. This great thing was supposed to make a theologian of him. It was a massive heirloom weighing about one hundred pounds: a throne upholstered in thick plush.

"What did he want? Suckerfish, I mean."

Gunnar looked from Lars to the letter, which he then slipped into a drawer cautiously, almost gently.

"He came to snoop around."

"Yes, but Rosen's—"

"Not Rosen this time. They know Rosen's gone. No, it's us, Lars."

"Us?"

Gunnar leaned back.

"I don't know, maybe they're only guessing. After all, that's their job. The gestapo came up to school, remember? It can't be so difficult to make a list of likely people. I'd use the elimination method myself."

Lars rose and sat on the edge of Gunnar's desk.

"Unless someone's been talking," continued Gunnar calmly.

"Are you thinking of Søren?"

"Søren won't say anything. He's OK."

"What about Junkersen? Or Dr. Halling?"

Gunnar sighed and put his legs up on the desk.

"Could be," he said. "Could be."

Lars prowled around the room, inspecting the leather-bound books. Everything ready for Gunnar's studies. Gunnar was swinging his legs down when Lars said, "But they can't prove anything, can they?"

"Prove anything? How naive can you get? The gestapo aren't interested in proof. They condemn people on suspicion alone. Not to mention the fact that we'd all talk the moment they brought out the instruments."

"What do you mean?"

"They tear people's nails out, Lars. They stub out their cigarettes on your bare flesh. They keep you awake around the clock. Bombard you with questions. Until finally you're willing to confess to anything just so long as they'll stop. You'll confess it was you put a bomb under Adolf Hitler in Berlin, and injected strychnine into Göring's layer cake, and poured insecticide into Mussolini's coffee, if that's what they want."

Lars smiled, but he was quickly serious again, because Gunnar himself was utterly serious. He meant every word. It didn't seem to make him any less determined—if anything, the opposite, even though he said they must continue to lie low, a message he expected Lars to pass on to Otto.

"So long as we aren't giving up for good," murmured Lars, toying with the books on the shelf.

Gunnar lit his corncob pipe.

"No," he said firmly, "we aren't giving up. We'll never give up. The sirens may wail all over town, but we'll wait. We'll wait for our train."

Lars nodded gloomily. He was on his way to the door when Gunnar said, "Lars, there's—there's something else I'd like to talk to you about."

Lars stood there with his hand on the doorknob. Here we go, he thought, now for the interrogation. Now it's all about to come out. Strip your clothes off, sit in the light, hands on the table. Answer precisely and clearly.

Lars sat down in the armchair again. Gunnar avoided his eyes. He seemed uneasy.

"You see, in a way I know you better than anyone else," he said. "And—well, I don't know, but when you and Kirsten got together—"

"We didn't get together. Not really."

"No, but didn't you like her?"

"Yes, I suppose so."

"Would you call it . . . love?"

Lars didn't answer. He wished he was somewhere else. A long way off. The room shrank. This was serious. This hurt.

"Well, no, I wouldn't. Why?"

"Because . . . oh, well. Then you've never been really, seriously in love?"

Lars said it was hard to tell.

Gunnar shook his head, talking to himself. "No," he said, "it's something you know absolutely for certain, right inside yourself. It simmers away there and you feel happy, and then the next moment—"

Gunnar pulled the top drawer out and put his letter on the desk. Lars muttered that it was late.

"I've written this about a thousand times," said Gunnar. "It's been lying here for weeks. I can't bring myself to send it."

Now he was looking straight at Lars, bewilderment in his eyes. An unhappy angel. This is wholly unnecessary, thought Lars, and ridiculously unfair.

"First there was all that about getting engaged at the regatta."

"Gunnar—"

"She kept putting me off. Keeping me at arm's length. I told myself it couldn't go on like that. I wanted to get a proper answer out of her. Irene's an honest girl. But then I kept putting it off myself. I didn't dare ask her straight out. I knew, deep down inside, I couldn't—I can't—do without her."

Lars looked at his brother, who had placed one clenched hand on the letter.

"You won't have to, Gunnar," he murmured.

Gunnar looked at him, almost gratefully.

"The problem is," he said unhappily, in a low voice, "she may have—well, I don't know, but she may have met someone else. I just have a kind of feeling about it. It's instinct. Maybe she just wants to wait and see how things turn out. I've— I've written all this in the letter. But I may have put it clumsily. I wondered if you'd read it?"

Lars looked him straight in the eye and shook his head violently.

"No, Gunnar," he whispered. "It's your business and no one else's."

"But—"

"And anyway there's something I have to tell you. Something I've been—well, keeping from you, for quite some time now."

Gunnar gave him a small incredulous smile. As if he couldn't possibly imagine Lars—his own little brother— doing anything bad. "Well, what is it?"

Lars looked up at the ceiling and was just taking a deep breath when there was a knock at the door. Gunnar rose heavily to his feet and opened it. Their father stood outside in his smoking jacket.

"I saw a light on," he said, nodding to Lars. He sat down in the best chair.

It occurred to Lars that this was possibly the first time the three of them had been alone together. Particularly so late at night. It was unusual for their father to be up after midnight.

"You know the gestapo were here today?" he began, clearly ill at ease. "Mother and I thought it was about Filip Rosen. But that man—Svend Hansen—had brought some copies of the local paper. About sabotage here in this town. He said he wanted to protect innocent Danish people, but that would require their willing cooperation. I've no idea exactly what he had in mind—he's a strange man—but after he left I went up to the church loft. So yes, I've seen your flag and the Nazi badges, but it didn't stop there, did it, Gunnar?"

Gunnar looked down.

"And I suddenly had a terrible idea. Almost like a vision."

Reverend Balstrup slipped his hand in his jacket pocket, took the Luger out, and put it on the desk. There it lay. Large as life, admitting no argument. With a history leading straight back to the old café in the woods and Otto Hvidemann from the Kolstrup Brickyard.

"Just what is going on?" asked their father, looking at Gunnar.

"I—I can't tell you," answered Gunnar impassively.

Father stared at Lars. Then he turned back to Gunnar. "Have you all gone mad? Do you know what you're risking? Answer me, Gunnar!"

"Yes. We know the risks."

"Do you? Do you, Gunnar? Don't get me wrong: I hate the Germans; I hate National Socialism. So do we all."

"Er—Junkersen and a good many others—," Lars began.

Father interrupted him brusquely. "There'll always be people like that, even in peacetime. I mean all the rest of us. Ordinary Danish men and women hate and despise Nazi Germany. That's why we're at war. So are England and France. But soldiers do the fighting. That's a soldier's job, after all. And one day this madness will end. Gunnar, look at me— you're not about to stop Rommel or Göring."

"It's our freedom that matters," said Gunnar quietly.

"Yes," shouted Father—Father, who never raised his voice—"your freedom and your lives."

They looked at each other.

"I want you to give me your word, Gunnar. I want you to promise me that from now on you and your friends will cease any kind of—"

"I can't do that."

"What did you say?"

"I said I can't do that. Father."

The last word was spoken softly and with regret.

Their father put his hand to his forehead and closed his eyes. "Maybe I'm just being selfish," he murmured, "but why you?"

"Someone has to start," said Lars.

"You mean, someone has to sacrifice himself?"

Lars looked down. In his heart, he thought both his father and Gunnar were right. Gunnar put the Luger away. In the drawer, with the letter.

Father went over to the door. He looked at them gravely but lovingly. Then he nodded wearily and went out.

There was a long silence. Finally Gunnar said, "I feel sorry for him."

Lars said he was exhausted, and opened the door into the dark hallway.

"Lars!"

Gunnar came out with him and laid a hand gently on his shoulder.

"Didn't you want to tell me something?"

Lars nodded, beginning to retreat toward his room.

"Oh, yes," he said. "About Otto's mother. She sleeps with Germans."

He lay in bed, tossing and turning. Judas, he thought. Traitor. First you steal Gunnar's girlfriend, then you gossip about Otto. Treachery upon treachery. Stretching on and on, until finally you're right out there where everything comes to an end, and the earth itself is gone and you're in free-fall.

WINTER

1942

SEVENTEEN

The first snow fell right on time, early in December. The town wrapped itself in its powdery blanket and snuggled down around the church. People had been looking forward to spending December and Christmas in the warmth and shelter of their own community. They put on their slippers, belted their woolly bathrobes, and settled in with the local newspaper.

At school, the principal lit the lights on the big tree in the main hall. It was a tradition, something that had to be done at this time of the year.

Lars had discovered a new side to himself—or, rather, two. Maybe there were only the two. Two profiles, hostile to each other; a Janus head, unaccountable even to Lars himself.

"I'll have to find the strength to control them," he whispered to himself in his cold bedroom. His two faces. His two voices.

One afraid, the other brave. One thoughtful, the other rash. Love and hate. His conscience hovered over the inaccessible landscape of his mind like a bird of prey, pecking and hacking at him, pestering and tormenting him.

Perhaps that was why he took to cycling out more and more frequently to the shanty settlement at the Kolstrup Brickyard, where one day was just like another, and Otto and his routine existence could soothe him. Otto Hvidemann steered his course by his own sextant. Or maybe he was following a course he had set for himself by stars Lars would never sight at all, let alone understand. Still, it was a welcome resting place.

A calm: a brief respite before the ice floe reached the falls. Because they all knew it would come: Lars, Otto, Luffe, Gunnar, and Axel. It was bound to come, like lightning from a clear sky. They had given themselves an ultimatum that seemed incomprehensible, but final. Crazy but necessary, jabbered his two heads.

Meanwhile they didn't hold many meetings, and they seldom went up to the loft. The shadow of the gestapo hovered ominously above them. Some people claimed Suckerfish had left town, until he suddenly turned up on the church porch the afternoon Lars and Gunnar were fitting new candles to the pews. They stood there with candles in their hands, feeling almost as though they had been caught in some guilty act. Svend Hansen was a master of innuendo, a complex man who had perfected his impassive facial expression over the years.

Where would he be but for the war? Who would he be without his Nazi badge and his black cap? Where would the war itself be without Suckerfishes?

He gave the Balstrups a rather sour smile. A mere twist of the lips. Maybe a smile like that required a lot of practice. Maybe Hitler's weird ideas and the thought of the battlefield and the Third Reich weren't really what appealed to him after all. Maybe he liked the novelty of seeing the reaction in people's faces: the fear in their eyes, the power and authority he wielded, the feelings he aroused.

"Balstrup," he said quietly. "A distinguished name."

Gunnar and Lars exchanged glances.

"Generation after generation, scholars, good Christians, a pure line."

"Can we help you?" Gunnar spoke with authority, sounding friendly without being obsequious.

Suckerfish stationed himself in front of Gunnar. They were the same height. The angel and the tormentor: an eternal couple. The same story over and over, down through the centuries. They looked into each other's eyes like two duelists at dawn. They both knew what it was about. They knew they were enemies and nothing in the world could alter that, not at any price. Svend Hansen's lips narrowed. He lifted his chin and appraised Gunnar through half-closed eyes.

"You're a talented young man, you know, Gunnar Balstrup," he said. "A man with a great future ahead of you. If you want it. A man your country could be proud of. Do you feel Danish, Gunnar Balstrup?"

"Yes," replied Gunnar hoarsely. "Yes, I feel Danish."

"Good. Good, Gunnar. That's just as it should be. A pure line. We can afford to be proud. Proud of belonging to the purest race of all."

Gunnar glanced briefly at Lars.

"It's only right for us to fight for the final supremacy, seeing that we're the master race. As we most certainly are, Gunnar. If we don't fight, we risk being overrun by rats. Black, yellow, brown, red. They increase and multiply, they breed, they mingle their blood. So how will things be for the pure Aryan race if we don't do anything? If we don't put a stop to it now?"

The gestapo man turned briskly and looked at Lars, who jumped involuntarily.

"Little brother Lars too. What riches! What possibilities! Two athletes, two good minds. There'll be a use for both of you."

The gestapo man's long thin fingers grazed the stack of hymnals Lars was holding. Maybe he was filing his nails before the torture. The door opened. In came Luffe, out of breath and wearing a wide smile, a smile that disappeared as soon as he caught sight of the gestapo man, who looked him up and down. Suckerfish let his glance wander from Luffe to Lars to Gunnar, where it finally came to rest.

Something was happening to the man's nostrils. His eyes took on a metallic gleam. His upper lip curled like a pig's snout; his nose dilated. The beast had scented prey. He bared his teeth, which were irregular and discolored. Gradually, he backed toward the door, nodding.

"Fight for all you hold dear, even if it means death," he said in a low voice, keeping his eyes on Gunnar, who looked away.

He opened the door for a second time. It was dark and cold outside. A blue shadow fell into the church.

"Strikes me," said Svend Hansen cheerfully, "the organ here in St. Petri sounds better these days."

Once he had gone, Gunnar and Lars collapsed into the uncomfortable wooden pews as if they had just been for a long run. Luffe asked what in hell was going on.

"The man's insane. Completely crazy," said Gunnar.

Lars rose to his feet. "He was warning us."

"What for?" asked Luffe.

"Because that's the part of his filthy job he enjoys," said Lars, irritated. "There's no doubt about it, Gunnar: The searchlight's right on us."

Gunnar nodded. "Yes, the searchlight's on us." He looked at the candles with a wooden expression, wholly unsuitable for an angel. Lars had seen him look like that before. In the school yard, sitting on a bench beside Irene. She had been wearing gloves and a ski cap, all hand-knitted. Her nose was red. A little cloud of vapor rose from her coral-colored mouth as she talked and laughed lightheartedly. But Gunnar just sat there looking wooden, hardly listening. It was a scene Lars had seen replayed at home. Irene's visits had become less frequent. The Balstrup family put it down to homework. She had changed too. She spoke in a high, rather shrill voice and laughed too much, often at nothing. Gunnar would sit beside her, and when it was time for her to leave and he saw her to the door and waved good-bye, he seemed almost relieved. *We are drifting on the treacherous ocean of concealment,* Lars had written in an exercise book.

Luffe snapped his fingers. "The twenty-second of December," he said.

Gunnar looked up. Lars put the hymnals down. Far away, muffled by the snow now, the German military band was marching through town.

"It's dead certain. They're switching the freight schedule around that evening, just for that train."

Gunnar nodded and smiled briefly at Lars. "We have nineteen days."

Gleeful anticipation animated Luffe's features. He raised his fists and laughed at the serious Gunnar, who stood up without noticing.

After dinner, as Lars opened the door to his room, he repeated it to himself: "We have nineteen days."

The radio was piping and whistling in the living room as his father tried to tune in the BBC. Gunnar was over at Luffe's. Lars was to take word to Otto the next day, and in five days' time they would all meet in the loft.

The loft was lit by church candles standing on shelves and rafters. The place was gloomy enough anyway, and the candles made it even more shadowy and menacing. The sounds of winter were entrenched now, like a dank substance seeping through the whole tower. Outside, the wind whistled, making the woodwork and rafters creak. A chorus in a minor key, distinctly wintry music.

The posters, caps, and pennants were gone; the last license plate had been thrown out, so it seemed natural also to drop the rituals they had once observed. There was no need to sing either the Danish or the Norwegian national anthem in cheerful student style. Even the sense that the group's existence was based on tradition had been replaced by a feeling that each of them had a job to do. *We see ourselves as a five-man squad,* Lars wrote in his exercise book, *but the fact is we're moving blindly with a current that is stronger than we are.*

Gunnar began by poisoning the atmosphere with his corn-cob pipe. He judiciously examined the large white piece of cardboard lying on the table. It was a detailed map of a stretch of railroad four and a half miles long, winding its way up from the south through the woods and taking a slight curve before reaching its last nine hundred yards outside town. A map with red circles: Luffe's map of operations.

Axel sat upright on his chair, looking pale but composed. Did he wish he was out of it now? Lars wondered. Would he heave a sigh of relief if Gunnar called the whole thing off and suggested going to a party with the girls from school instead? Axel hadn't said anything; it was just that fixed, attentive look on his face.

Luffe had lost his giggle. He was surveying his own work. A theoretician, with a theoretical approach to life. Maybe he'd never get a proper grasp on real life; maybe you had to preserve a certain distance from it if you were Luffe. As if everything were just an interesting illusion. Otto was silent as ever. He was waiting. Waiting for the day, waiting for the signal. And meanwhile he was preparing himself. Steady and uncompromising, that was Otto. He might be one of the group now, but he was still essentially a loner.

Lars glanced up. Gunnar had been saying something about a problem. He spoke in a low, expressionless voice, without any emotion or color, as if he were alone.

And perhaps that was the truth of it, when all was said and done. They were all alone. Søren's function had been to hold them together, remind them of their ideals, place them in a regular, well-ordered hierarchy.

Gunnar was talking about the gestapo and the way Svend Hansen kept turning up in and out of season: at the rectory, in church, at the rowing club.

"The pig's picked up a scent," muttered Luffe.

Gunnar nodded. "He knows something. I may be wrong, but my instinct tells me someone's informed on us. As far as I can see, there are just the two possibilities, but you never know. There's Junkersen, and there's Kirsten's father."

Lars had to tell Otto who Junkersen was.

"And there's something else," Gunnar went on. "I keep feeling that there's something I've overlooked."

Axel said surely it made no sense for the gestapo to hang back if they had any evidence to go on. If they were sure.

"They know something," said Gunnar, "but not enough. They can't nail us just like that. Or rather they don't want to. They want to catch us in the act. That way they can hold us up as an example and a warning, so we'll be blamed for the revenge they take, and the town will turn against us, not them."

"So in that case, what about all this?" asked Lars, pointing at the map.

"That's why we're having this meeting," said Gunnar. "The

whole thing's ready. We know for certain now that the train's coming through on December twenty-second. We know exactly when, and we know it will be carrying the freight we discussed before: the tanks, the war material being sent to Norway. We know when, how, and where to deploy ourselves. But first there's this problem we have with Suckerfish. And that damn hunch of mine, that—that damn gut feeling that there's something I've overlooked."

"Well then?" asked Lars, raising his voice. "So we know the gestapo have their eye on us, we know we've given ourselves away to Kirsten's father, and we most certainly know Junkersen's a Nazi sympathizer. In which case, is it very smart to mount such a drastic operation just now?"

Gunnar looked straight at him. "Why don't you answer that yourself?"

Lars drew back, feeling ill at ease. "Why ask just me?" Gunnar's glance seemed like an accusation. He longed to say he had no intention of throwing his life away for the sake of a train; he felt he had too much to lose. But then again— oh, yes, then again he could always hear the arguments against such an attitude echoing in his mind. It had to be done. By someone. No way around that.

Axel cleared his throat. Luffe pointed out that the details of the plan provided them with some kind of safety net: They'd taken most contingencies into account, and he personally was in favor of going through with it. Maybe Luffe wasn't so theoretical after all. So where did Gunnar stand? Watching his brother, Lars came to the conclusion that Gunnar himself wasn't sure.

"How about you, Otto?" Gunnar asked, casting a friendly glance at Otto. Otto looked artlessly back at him, as if he had only just this moment woken up.

"Oh, well—well, yes."

"Yes what?"

"Yes, I'm in favor," Otto said.

"What about the gestapo?" asked Gunnar. "And all these things we've been discussing? Suppose someone's informed on us?"

Otto looked from one to another of them and shrugged his shoulders. "Then that's the way it is," he said quietly.

Gunnar looked hard at Otto. Lars smiled. Oh, forget it, Gunnar, he thought, you'll never get to understand him. Luffe asked Axel what he thought. Axel said he wouldn't go against a majority vote.

Gunnar turned to Lars.

"You don't have to," he said.

Lars looked at the set of pulleys that held up the enormous chandelier, and he remembered listening to Rosen's joyous organ music. The plaster was flaking away. He was swearing the oath. He had waited so long to become a member of the St. Petri Group. And now, at last, he'd made it.

"I suppose this is what we've always wanted," he said. "If we really mean any of what we say. But I have to admit I'm terrified."

Axel smiled with relief.

"OK." Gunnar brought his hand down on the table. "OK. December twenty-second, just after ten at night. The day of the Christmas dance up at school, with the play and the school orchestra and all that. The Christmas party will provide our alibi."

"But surely we won't be there?" Lars interrupted.

"Yes, we will. I'm just coming to that. I know it'll be a bit different for you, Otto, because you don't go to our school."

Otto stroked his upper lip.

"But the rest of us," continued Gunnar, "Axel, Luffe, Lars, and yours truly, will be up there onstage as expected. The principal's written the play himself; he always does. It's about the three wise men from the East this year."

"Look, Gunnar," said Lars, "wouldn't it be a good idea for you and Luffe to let the rest of us know exactly what your plan is? How can we be onstage and out in the woods at the same time?"

Gunnar waved this suggestion aside. "We leave here in a couple of minutes," he said firmly, "and we don't meet again until seven P.M. on the twenty-first, up here. If you see my bike standing by the side door to the tower, you all go home again. If you don't see it, then we'll hold our last meeting of the year. You'll get your instructions before that. On the twenty-second, until nine-thirty, Otto will stay home and the rest of us will be at school. Meanwhile we act as if we hardly know one another. Is that understood?"

Axel nodded vigorously. Otto looked away.

Gunnar scraped the ashes out of his pipe and glanced at Luffe, who grinned broadly, as if he were having his photograph taken. For no apparent reason.

EIGHTEEN

As a rule, the principal's Christmas play was a traditional musical with a lively, slightly satirical moral, a fast-moving plot, and plenty of songs. It was entertaining, but it contained a serious message as well. Particularly this year, when the biblical subject was also an allegory for the present-day troubles. The Three Kings poked fun at Hitler, whose only converts to Nazism were a flock of sheep. The sheep also acted as a bleating chorus.

All through December they held singing auditions, picked actors, rehearsed, and painted scenery. Irene took the part of one of the Three Kings and Søren played another, while Gunnar, Axel, Luffe, and Lars arranged to be in the chorus, wearing woolly sheep costumes. Everything was working out just the way they wanted.

The last rehearsals were over. The performance itself, then Christmas and vacation, lay ahead. Gunnar delivered the final instructions to the group and made secret arrangements with four other people in his class; those four also memorized the songs for the chorus.

Lars went to see Otto on December twenty-first. It was a clear, frosty day with a pale blue sky. The freezing mist had lifted, and delicate pastel colors muted the white of the snow glimmering on the usually drab stretch of meadowland.

Otto repeated his final instructions. He was even quieter than normal. The plan was for him and Lars to arrive a little after the others tomorrow evening. Axel was going to bike down to the viaduct by himself and act as lookout, while Gunnar and Luffe took up positions near the stretch of railroad between the woods and the town. Lars and Otto were to be strategically placed on either side of the tracks, keeping an eye on the nearby road and bicycle path.

It sounded so simple and straightforward. Just press a switch, and boom! The freight train topples over, and the bold saboteurs escape into the dark. Ahead of them lies euphoria, the triumphant victory wail of the brewery sirens, conspiratorial glances exchanged as they walk hand in hand around the tree on Christmas Eve. Then relief and peace and quiet until the New Year, when they'll prepare to face A.D. 1943, the year when the Allies absolutely *must* succeed in both the East and North Africa.

Life *must* return to normal, to laughter and fun. But when Lars thought of the soldiers marching through town, when he saw the stamp of Nazi influence on newspapers, radio, and movies, and when he heard Svend Hansen's perverted monologue about the purest race of all, over and over again he felt nausea rise in his throat. He actually couldn't breathe. A sense of disgust and loathing lay like a knot in his stomach, a knot of fear that made him clench his teeth and suppress his anxious misgivings.

As Gunnar was always saying, someone has to go first, someone has to do it, whatever it costs; then other people will follow. Good Danes, brave men and women. The resistance movement would be organized from both Copenhagen and London. Germany would realize Denmark had not capitulated. Lars could work himself up to a fever pitch on this subject, rocking back and forth in almost rhythmical preparation, concentrating both body and mind on a single idea. All other considerations were gone: school, the future, love, need. Just one image remained, a picture that couldn't be erased from his mind even if they sent him to the eastern front. If only Rosen could share in the moment of exaltation.

He walked across the cold meadow with Otto, who was wearing five woolly undershirts with a layer of newspapers tied around his middle. He looked like a Russian shepherd.

"We stand around in our sheep costumes," Lars explained, with a slightly hysterical laugh, "singing the principal's own little allegorical songs and swinging our legs. It's the principal's private gesture of defiance, if you ask me. The audience can go home after the show feeling they've done something good just by laughing and clapping. Still, maybe there's some point to it."

Otto didn't answer. He clearly couldn't care less about allegorical musicals featuring schoolboys and schoolgirls dressed up as sheep. He had some pebbles in his hands and was absently tossing them in the air.

Meanwhile Lars saw Irene appear in his mind, wearing her crown of golden cardboard, a mustache, and a sky blue cloak. She was smiling at everyone. It was like a lamp being lit; she was the natural center point, where the light was most brilliant. She said something to Gunnar as Lars stood not far off. She was teasing Gunnar, but he didn't react, and Irene turned the light out again.

She knew that Gunnar couldn't accept the fine gradation of feeling that had turned their love into friendship. It had to be all or nothing. Once, Lars had spoken with her of the changes in Gunnar. It was a different Gunnar now, completely different. The transformation had taken place swiftly and smoothly, and now the metamorphosis was complete. The question was, did they know anything at all about this new Gunnar? He was always smiling and laughing, yes, but only after deciding to do so, announcing his intentions, as it were. His spontaneity was gone, that golden aura he used to have. It was as if he'd traveled through purgatory and singed his wings.

One evening after dinner, when they had been sitting by the radio, the new organist, Alfred Johansen, had asked what Gunnar planned to do following his final exams. Mother had answered, looking proudly at her elder son, that he was planning to study theology. Gunnar was sitting where he usually sat, next to Father, who had his precious atlas on his knees.

It showed the battlefields, in color, among the brown mountains and green valleys. The towns were red dots, the rivers black, the railroads broken lines, the deserts yellow, and the lakes blue. But the atlas was out-of-date, like all atlases now. The borders were no longer accurate. The good thing about the atlas, on the other hand, was that you couldn't actually see weeping human beings in the small circular blobs marking Paris, Berlin, London, and Bristol; you couldn't see cities bombed to ruins, or homeless people, or the maimed and the dead. There were no U-boats or destroyers in the sky blue seas. The world was as it used to be.

Unlike Gunnar, who suddenly said, "Things have changed."

It took a little time for his words to sink in. And it was not his father's atlas he was referring to. The minister raised his head.

"What did you say, my boy?"

"I said things have changed." Over by the desk in the corner, Gunnar lit his corncob pipe.

"What do you mean, changed?" Mother laughed nervously.

Poor Mother, thought Lars, poor dear, kind, credulous Mother. The war is coming into your own home now, and you'll have to look it in the face, however ugly it may be. Iodine, bandages, and chamomile tea won't do any good now. You can preserve all the berries you like, you can sew and mend and make clothes over and ignore it, but the war is here, right here in your house, saying: Things have changed.

Poor Alfred Johansen breathed on his rimless spectacles

and turned an innocent, childlike face on Gunnar as he asked, well-meaningly, what other subject Gunnar meant to study. He had no idea what this was really all about; it would have been too much to expect that he would.

"I'm not planning to study anything," said Gunnar. "I want to travel."

Lars glanced at his father, who was frowning and paying an unusual amount of attention to the conversation. But he didn't say anything, and it was difficult to tell how much surprise or even shock he felt. Perhaps he recognized the new Gunnar. Perhaps the new Gunnar touched a familiar chord in the minister himself. Meanwhile Mother smiled with relief and waved a hand at Gunnar as if to say that now she knew he wasn't being serious. If there was anyone who could pull the rug out from under Mother it was Gunnar, and now he'd done it, and with both hands.

Come on, Gunnar, thought Lars impatiently, get it over with, get her on the move. It's about time she woke up. She's OK once you reach bottom, but you have to drag her down there first. However, before the news from London came on, Gunnar rose and walked across the room without looking at anyone. As he put his hand on the door, Father asked with forced mildness, "Do you mean that, Gunnar?"

"Yes, I do," said Gunnar, and left without turning around.

After that, even Møller, the exiled Danish patriot, sounded a little flat on the radio. Johansen said young people sometimes got strange ideas in their heads. Why, his own sister suddenly went off to Gotland in 1936 to collect rocks!

The discussion of Johansen's sister, who in fact sounded

perfectly normal, went on for nearly a quarter of an hour and reinforced the general impression of the Johansen family as conformists. The moral, or rather the point, of the story was that after staying away for all of three months, the rebellious sister came home, got her teacher's certificate, married a school administrator, and had twins.

Mother sat with Father's imitation wool jacket on her lap.

"Yes, but this isn't like our Gunnar," she murmured.

"No," sighed Father, "it's not, my friend. And this isn't just some strange idea of his. No, I'm afraid we've only had 'our Gunnar' on loan."

Mother's gaze swung around, like a bright beam of light, and she looked at Lars as if seeing him for the very first time. As if she were saying: What will happen next? I only have you now, little Lars.

The next day he had cycled out to the fjord.

It was early December, and the snow was still soft and white, just as snow ought to be. They were standing by the partly frozen water. Irene and her friend Anna. They'd almost finished making their snowman. He had two lumps of coal for eyes and a carrot for a nose. Irene's ski cap sat on his big head, tilted saucily to one side.

When Lars wheeled his bike toward them, Anna walked away.

Irene looked at him with a small chilled smile. Lars was aware of his heart thumping and his legs trembling. As if they hadn't seen each other for five long years. Looking so lovely oughtn't to be allowed. Beautiful and dreamy, with that hesitant smile. So much life and happiness frozen inside.

"Nice, isn't he?" She pointed at her snowman.

Lars nodded. "But it's going to thaw soon."

She looked up at the sky. It's the way she moves, he thought, that's what I loved first, before anything else. Her sudden movements, brusque and unexpectedly elegant. A certain gawkiness, even.

"That's why I made him," she said. "Now I can see him on my way to school every morning in the dark. I can watch him quietly melt away."

"That's a funny thing to do," said Lars, breaking into unmusical laughter.

The sun was setting. The last of its rays struck her forehead.

"If I were the last sunbeam that's where I'd rest too," he said quietly.

"Last sunbeam?"

Only then did he realize he had been thinking out loud. He muttered something about the dark winter nights and how the days would soon be longer again. If she hadn't interrupted him, he could have rambled on about the changing seasons until springtime.

"Will you be staying for the dance afterward?" she asked casually. "After the play, I mean?"

Her gloved hand was resting on the handlebars of his bike. Lars stared at his ski boots, his gray checked socks, and his brown knee pants.

"If I can," he murmured.

She took her hand out of the glove. Her fingers were red with the cold and the snow. One crooked forefinger ran slowly down his face. From his forehead, past his mouth, down to the point of his chin. She followed its course with her eyes as if it were a tear.

Then she put her hand carefully back into its glove.

Lars smiled gently at her as she picked up her bike.

"It's a shame about the snowman," he said quietly.

"I can always make another." She smiled, blinking her eyes. And then she was gone.

Otto kicked a bit of rubble. It seemed to hurt his toes. Lars took him by the shoulders and made him turn so that they were facing each other. "Do you ever remember anything people tell you?" he asked.

"Yes, sure," said Otto, without much conviction.

"About me being in love with Gunnar's girlfriend—do you remember that?"

Otto did not reply, but took a licorice stick out of his pocket and began chewing it as he studied Lars with mild surprise.

"Gunnar's girlfriend," repeated Lars. "Well, you know something? She's in love with me too. How about that, Otto?"

Otto chewed more energetically, then removed the licorice stick from his mouth and looked at it disapprovingly.

"So is she your girlfriend now?" he asked, spitting a shred of licorice out.

Lars looked at him hard and smiled. "You know something else, Otto? You're my best friend."

"I am?"

"You are. Definitely my best friend."

Otto nodded without taking his eyes off Lars, before concentrating on the licorice stick again. "The Germans were up at our place on Monday," he said.

Lars removed his hand from Otto's shoulder as if he had burned himself.

"What—what did they want?"

"Wanted to snoop around. The one you all call Suckerfish was with them. That long, thin fellow."

Lars looked out at the fjord, where he saw nothing but infinity. Suckerfish! This was not good news. Not at all.

"Did he say anything?"

"He said I might get a reward if I helped him."

Lars stared at Otto, who had begun on the other end of the black stick.

"So what did you say?"

"I asked how much the reward was."

Lars hesitated. "You—you asked how much the reward was?"

"He wouldn't say, though. Said it depended what I had for him."

Lars placed himself in front of Otto. "Why do you think he came to see you, of all people? Have you thought about that? He might have picked a hundred and seventeen others, but he didn't pick any of those hundred and seventeen others, he picked you."

Otto was watching the little ferry making its way across the fjord. "I'd like to cut *him* down to size," he muttered.

"Good idea."

They went back to the shanty settlement and hung around

Otto's front door for a while. Lars was in a state of indecision. He didn't know how to say what he was thinking, or even what he wanted to say. But as Lars swung his leg over the crossbar of his bike, Otto remarked casually, "My mother isn't waitressing anymore."

As so often before, Lars lay on his bed, unable to relax. He could really have used a good night's sleep. Gunnar was lying not far away, just down the hall, or so Lars supposed. Maybe he was sleeping like a log. Sleeping the sleep of the just. Or maybe he was lying there like Lars, staring up at the ceiling and hearing nothing. Why didn't they talk to each other anymore, apart from saying what was absolutely necessary? There are quite a few things he's never told me, thought Lars. Secrets. Things the new Gunnar doesn't tell people. Of course, I could go to his room.

He closed his eyes and felt the effects of the wine on his system again. He wasn't used to drinking three glasses of red wine in quick succession. When he closed his eyes he saw the others before him at the meeting they had just held. Gunnar at the end of the table, serious, rather commanding. The wine he poured into long-stemmed glasses hadn't made them cheerful. Lars hadn't seen the decanter before. Luffe rose to his feet and proposed an elaborate toast to their operation, but the general feeling was somber. Axel was silent, and Otto made a face when he swallowed.

There was not much to say. Not now. Maybe that was why Gunnar suggested they all take hands. It felt a little odd, and Luffe had giggled, but still it was good to be holding hands with Axel and Otto. Feeling their warmth, knowing they all stood together, shoulder to shoulder. Then Gunnar and Luffe began stamping on the floor. Axel joined in, then Lars, and finally Otto. Stamp, stamp, stamp . . . the rhythm, the ritual, the pulse of it.

"What . . . will we . . . do with . . . Göring?" yelled Gunnar, pale in the face.

Stamp, stamp, stamp . . .

"First we grab old Göring
By his big fat calves.
Then we knock down Goebbels—
We don't do things by halves!"

The big school hall was decorated with colored lights and branches of evergreens bearing the dannebrog. The principal was so nervous that his whole face was blotchy. Mrs. Hartmann sat down at the piano. The audience had not arrived yet, but the actors, extras, and chorus had been ready for quite some time. Four substitute sheep were sitting in the dressing room passing a cigarette around. The janitor and his assistant sat at the entrance. Now the first spectators began to trickle in.

We'll dangle Hitler from a rope
And right beside him Ribbentrop. . . .

The Three Kings were receiving their final touches of makeup. Irene looked inquiringly at Lars, but turned away when Luffe and Gunnar appeared in their sheep costumes. The principal took his place in the prompter's box. Every seat in the hall was occupied. A murmur of expectation traveled across the audience like a swarm of bees, dying away when the lights went down.

> Look how stupid, all in line,
> One, two, three, four Nazi swine!

The end of the first act: applause and curtain. Everything was going according to plan. Gunnar propelled Luffe off to one side of the stage. Luffe tapped Axel on the shoulder. Lars went down to the dressing room and took his sheep costume off. Gunnar checked his watch. Axel went out. The door clicked shut.

Onstage, the second act began. It was a couple of minutes before the chorus entered.

Lars bicycled through the dark town on his way to the Kolstrup Brickyard. He thought of the singing, the principal's simple play, and last night, when he had slept for only three hours. An uneasy sleep, troubled by many images, mostly of Gunnar as he used to know him: his big-hearted brother with the guileless smile. The angel from St. Petri.

"In whose shadow I grew up," he murmured as he biked around the corner.

Otto had tucked his sisters into bed. Lars stood in the hallway and watched him kiss them good night. He does that as if it were the most natural thing in the world, thought Lars. No clashes here, no harsh conflicts. Peace and quiet.

"Kylle's running a bit of a temperature," said Otto.

He wanted them to make a detour by way of the Central School, and they had to pedal hard. Lars nervously urged Otto to hurry, and then followed him through the doorway of the school.

There were five cleaning women at work. Otto's mother was in the middle of the wide linoleum staircase, a bucket to her left. Her hair was tied up in a bun. She was wearing blue overalls and no makeup and looked both fresher and younger. Otto tripped slightly, then ran up the nine steps to her. Only now did Lars understand what Otto was doing. Otto's mother looked at him and forced a small brave smile. Lars turned aside when she suddenly gave Otto a hug. Otto slipped out of it immediately and ran back down to Lars.

In a few minutes they were on their way through town. Axel was standing somewhere in the woods with a signal light. They bent low over their handlebars, speeding along dark paths. The trees flashed by, shadowy figures, extras in this drama: spruce, fir, and larch in a bracing wind. Lars sat upright on his bike. This is *our* woods, he thought, *our* trees, Danish roots, Danish soil down through the centuries, the fjord, the valley, the hills and meadows, all as old as time itself. And it's all a part of me.

Forty minutes to go. Otto overtook him. Lars saw his profile flash by. Was there something different about Otto this evening? Yes, there was: He's brushed his hair, thought Lars. His hands and nails are spotlessly clean. Good heavens. As if he was going to a party. Lars imagined Otto standing in front of a mirror, dipping a comb in water, his untidy hair rebelling but finally conquered. Otto taking out his cleanest socks and shirt. Was Hvidemann dressed for a church confirmation? No, too much of a loner for that. He cleans his boots, inspects their soles. A wedding, then? No, too somber for that. Then finally he's ready. He turns around slowly in front of the mirror. Ready for a funeral.

Forty minutes. The train was scheduled to appear in forty minutes, to come racing up over the hill. The metal tracks shone in the cold moonlight.

Lars and Otto threw down their bicycles. Otto ran across the tracks and took up his position opposite the tree where Lars had stationed himself.

He spotted Gunnar and Luffe, two bundles of clothes crouched by the tracks, doing something with explosive charges, wires, and primers. They were working fast and feverishly. Stooping low and carrying a wire fastened around some sort of reel, Gunnar ran down to the wooden box that held the master switch.

Luffe followed him, hiding the wire. Lars knew Luffe had been over the whole thing a million times, visualizing it, calculating—weighing, measuring, multiplying, dividing. To him, this was like a test, a problem on an exam. He hadn't made a big thing of it. He was a theoretician about to put something into practice. An unborn chick imagining the world outside. And now the chick was about to peck its way out, to test its theories. The shell was about to crack. "Welcome to the real world, Oluf," murmured Lars, standing close to the tree trunk and gazing up at the mighty Sitka spruce. Its majestic crown seemed to be watching for the northbound train.

Thirty minutes. He released the safety catch of the Luger, which was his now. Yes, things were going according to plan. He stared at the gun and realized he was freezing. The cold had crept into his bones. His blood was frozen and congealing. In thirty minutes' time he wouldn't be able to move at all. He exercised his fingers and squeezed the handle of the pistol. He remembered what Søren had once said, long ago. Sensible Søren, standing onstage now among the incense, gold, and myrrh. Lars hoped people were enjoying themselves. Well, the play was meant to be a comedy. The principal would be sweating away in the prompter's box while one of his pupils, Axel Terkelsen by name, was down here by the viaduct doing his duty.

A sense of duty is blind, deaf, and dumb; it just exists, like some invisible part of the body. Axel had always had one, relying heavily on it, using it as though it were an oracle speaking out of a hole in the ground, to which he could turn whenever in doubt. He could just lie flat on the ground and shout down to the oracle on duty. There was never any question about the answer. But now young Terkelsen, with his face that gave nothing away, now young Terkelsen did feel doubt, Lars supposed. He was freezing in the bitter cold by the viaduct, shuffling his feet and dancing around, thinking about his family at home. About his school friends, his little sister and the dollhouse he had made her for Christmas. All his own work.

Axel was a person who had never found life particularly complicated. He had been teased as a boy for being fat. But it was just baby fat. Everything passes, and Axel went with the flow. Now here he was standing by the viaduct with a signal light, watching, listening, frightened—badly frightened. Duty. Maybe one ought to argue with it. Duty speaks with many voices, right? Didn't he have a responsibility to his family? Suppose they knew he was standing here, involved in blowing up the railroad? Before leaving home, he had stood for some time looking at his mother, two rooms away, snipping at the arms of a jacket. For him. He was to wear it Christmas Eve, when they lit the lights on the tree. He had been sitting in the bathroom with his eyes closed, humming. The telephone had rung in the living room. It was his mother's sister from Copenhagen. The conversation was short. Oh, well, said his mother, they couldn't complain, they were doing all right here in the country; she offered to help if things became too bad in the capital. After she hung up, she was humming a popular song.

Axel's father had come home from the office. He was in a good mood, looking forward to Christmas and the school play. Axel's little sister teased him about his part as a sheep. Their parents hugged each other and laughed. His little sister stood on one leg and did a pirouette. Axel stared down into that oracular hole, where faces swept past, screaming. The many faces of duty, the two aspects of responsibility. I'm doing it for all of you, he told himself as he went out the door.

He had met Lars at school and told him how he felt, told him everything, in detail. Lars was a good listener. He said he understood. But Axel had more on his mind: his sister's dollhouse. Lars said this wasn't really a good time to discuss it, but Axel explained that he'd been working on that dollhouse for five months. It had three stories, counting the attic. He had cut and glued, sawed and filed, polished, stitched, and tacked. Making the living room, dining room, bathroom, little girl's bedroom, stairs, nursery, attic. Lars had turned his back to Axel and stepped into his sheep costume. Axel had just gone on talking.

"There's the father doll with his long pipe, sitting in the living room. And the mother doll is in the kitchen, cooking dinner, and the little girl doll, Agnes, is doing her hair up on the first floor, in braids like my sister's. She's called Agnes too. I've done so much work on that house. It's a faithful copy of our own house, that's the thing, you see."

"Could you just shut up a moment, Axel?"

"I've kept it all a secret, of course. I didn't want anyone to know anything, not even my parents."

Lars shook off the memory of Axel's voice. In thirty minutes, when Axel would come out the other side, he'd be a different person.

Luffe was down by the tracks again. Maybe he just wanted to check his masterpiece, or maybe there was something wrong. Gunnar was urging him to hurry.

Gunnar, who would hardly look anyone in the eye these days. Gunnar, their leader. Gunnar, who didn't want to study theology like his father and his even more famous grandfather, the stout Bishop of Viborg. So Gunnar wanted to travel now! What for? Well, to get away, of course. As far away as possible. Right out to the mangrove swamps. Out to the sultan's ruined palace overgrown with creepers, papaya entwining the balustrades. There goes Gunnar on horseback, cantering through shady orange groves. He's been warned against this place, but he has to go, he must. The palace was abandoned by its original inhabitants long ago; people say it's under a curse. But what difference do the rumors make to Gunnar Balstrup? He is urging Luffe on. Luffe is sitting on a little donkey and studying a phrase book. Gunnar makes his way up the steps and pushes the heavy door open. Cobwebs cling to him. On he goes, from hall to hall, farther and farther, until no voice from the outside can reach him. Then, at last, he's at his journey's end. He has finally found what he was looking for. Luffe is still sitting on the donkey when Gunnar emerges, smiling a warm, genial smile. He has his wings again.

"So you found them!" laughs Luffe. "What about the halo?"

"It was too heavy, old friend."

The theoretician, the dollhouse builder, the fallen angel —and Otto Hvidemann, the mortician. They were all waiting.

Lars was feeling a little warmer now. He saw Luffe hurry back to Gunnar, and they took cover. Otto had made himself invisible somewhere on the slopes of the railroad embankment, but Lars knew he was there, up to something in the dark.

Back at school the play must be over, and the actors would be acknowledging their well-earned ovation. Irene bowing. Søren bowing. All the sheep, including four fake ones, taking their bows as well. The principal emerging from the prompter's box, and over at the Central School a mop waving in the air like a great seabird over the Pacific Ocean. Kylle running a temperature. Agnes with her hair in braids. Irene taking off her long beard in front of a little mirror, looking past her own reflection in the glass. Five minutes to go . . .

Lars turned. Was that the train already? He looked over at the viaduct, where Axel's signal light should be flashing. He saw nothing. Luffe and Gunnar drew back in the undergrowth. Otto was still invisible. Waiting for the funeral. There was a sound, though. A sound coming from the woods. There it was again. Engines, motorbikes. A rumbling noise. Trucks. Yellow eyes showing through the spruce, fir, and pine. Lars threw a stone at the tracks as Gunnar came into view. Gunnar looked around, bewildered, and Luffe scrambled over to him. Lars was completely at a loss. All was still again. There was only the wind in the treetops. No, it certainly hadn't been the train. Gunnar and Luffe looked at each other and at the viaduct. They waited. Then the first shouts echoed through the woods, coming from all sides. A searchlight was switched on. Several lights showed. German voices cursed.

Gunnar ran, but Luffe hesitated, shifting from foot to foot. Something had happened to upset his calculations. The world was in disarray; he knew he could never go back to theorizing in the egg again. Gunnar grabbed hold of him. Was this the moment when he'd get his wings back? Lars rose to his feet. Where was Otto? He'd be waiting patiently for the coffin, the funeral procession, and the burial service. The first shots cracked through the night.

Gunnar shouted to Lars, who ran down to join him and Luffe.

"Come on, Luffe, for God's sake!" cried Gunnar desperately. "Give him a shove, Lars!" Gunnar was trying to get Luffe moving—Luffe, who couldn't figure out how all this could be happening—when Lars stopped dead. The light! The signal was flashing from the viaduct. The brave dollhouse maker was waving his light.

"The train's coming, Gunnar," muttered Luffe hoarsely, almost dreamily.

Gunnar pushed him hard in the back. There were more shots. More lights. More voices, shouted commands, and barking dogs.

Gunnar had managed to haul Luffe up the slope now. He turned to Lars, who was staring at the waving light. Axel could stop now. . . .

"Lars! What are you doing, for God's sake?"

Gunnar scrambled back down to him and took hold of his collar.

"Gunnar—"

"Someone's informed on us," gasped Gunnar. "Come on. We'll do what we arranged."

"What we arranged?"

"Go to the old café. What the hell's come over you? Lars!"

Lars stared at the locomotive roaring toward them around the curve. Smoke rose, rolling over the treetops.

"We have to go underground."

Lars looked at his brother, bewildered. Go underground. Get away, out of here. Perhaps—perhaps forever. His head was spinning.

"The old café, Lars! We'll scatter and meet up there."

"Gunnar. Gunnar, I have to go back."

"Back?"

"Yes, back. Back to school. I'll join you later."

"Are you crazy? Don't you realize . . . ?"

More shooting. The dark shadows were coming closer. Then Otto opened fire. Gunnar and Lars ducked down. Otto was shooting as though possessed.

The train snorted like an animal.

Gunnar looked imploringly at Lars, who answered him with a brief shake of his head. Gunnar looked away. Just for a split second, but perhaps long enough to see right into the sultan's palace.

"OK, Lars," he said quietly. "But take care of yourself."

Lars smiled and nodded. Gunnar gave him a quick hug and took three steps up the bank.

"And tell her good-bye for me," he said.

He was gone before the words sank in.

Lars stared at the train, paralyzed, calling down heartfelt curses upon it. On the other side of the tracks, flashes of fire spurted from Otto's gun. The Germans had taken up their positions. Lars raced up the slope to the left, where he had a view of the whole area. The place was swarming with soldiers. Then, suddenly, Otto came tearing across the tracks just thirty feet in front of the roaring locomotive.

"Otto," whispered Lars, "don't do it. Don't do it, Otto."

Shots rang out from the trees. Ten or twelve soldiers were running full out along the road to the embankment and then down the slope in pursuit of Otto, who was racing for Luffe's wooden box.

Gunnar had disappeared. So had Luffe, and Lars fervently hoped Axel was on his way home. Home to his dollhouse. Lars himself stayed put, holding his breath. Otto was running with slow, exaggerated strides, as if he were moving underwater. Here came the train, there were its lights, bright cones rising above the woods.

Tell her good-bye for me, Gunnar had said.

The soldiers took aim. They were very close now. What in hell did Otto think he was doing? Lars fired the pistol for the first time. Otto glanced up. Then the Germans opened fire with a vengeance, but Otto remained, waiting.

"Run! For heaven's sake, Otto, run!" shouted Lars as the train swept by. Through the smoke, he could see Otto put one foot on the switch Luffe had fitted to the box. The locomotive was a few yards away from the explosives. Otto waited. A second went by, and then the forest exploded. The tracks rose in the air, the ties splintered. Shards flew like projectiles, piercing the tree trunks where the soldiers were. But the train moved steadily on. Otto had disappeared; the noise died down. Only the massive locomotive pulling cars full of war material continued on its way in a long, dreamlike movement. And then, with an ear-splitting crash and a shrill howl, the train veered off course, tilted, and in an awe-inspiring chain reaction, toppled over on its side.

He was racing through the bushes, sweating and freezing at the same time. The blood was thumping feverishly in his temples. Come on, come on! He disregarded the pain in his legs and feet, his calves and thighs, pushing harder and harder, more and more desperately, on the pedals of his bike.

The school nestled there cozily, dimly lit. The play had ended long ago and the dance was in progress. He heard soft clarinets and the caramel tones of saxophones. Lars flung his bicycle down and raced in through a side door. Down to the dressing room. Not a soul there. Up the stairs. His breathing was labored. A small group of people stood outside the dance hall. Anna was among them. When she saw Lars, she ducked back in again. Noise poured out through the doorway. The sound of a party, with bright colors and laughter. He opened the door to the physics lab and sat down on a bench, feeling his fatigue hammer inside him. The door opened.

She was wearing her dark red skirt, and her hair was pinned up. She looks older, he thought.

"Lars . . ."

He took her hands. He kissed her fingertips. She stroked his hair with one hand and gently kissed him.

"It . . . it didn't work out quite the way we meant," he muttered. "Not exactly as we planned. But—well, you understand, Irene."

She kissed him over and over.

"I want you to know . . ."

She nodded. "I do know."

"And now I have to go."

"Why?" she whispered.

He pulled away from her, shaking his head. "I'll be back. I promise I will."

She took his head in her hands. All was still. He got to his feet, but his legs buckled under him.

"Oh, God. I am so tired."

Then the door opened again. Lars turned around. The ceiling light was switched on. Suckerfish was looking straight at him. Two officers and a group of soldiers stood behind the gestapo man.

"Lars Balstrup, you are under arrest!"

A fine meerschaum pipe, the color of amber, lay in Suckerfish's hand.

N I N E T E E N

When Lars next saw them, it was in the sunlit prison yard. Gunnar, Luffe, and Axel were lined up with their backs to the wall and their wrists handcuffed in front of them. Danish policemen, German soldiers, and a very formal police superintendent who was reading out something unintelligible were also in the yard.

It had taken Lars most of the night to reach a belated but consoling conclusion. When all was said and done, when all their escapades were considered and weighed, when the picture of Irene had been framed and put in place in his mind, he had no regrets on that day, December twenty-third, 1942.

Far from it.

He saw the same bright defiance in the eyes of Gunnar and Luffe, like a pilot light always burning, a fire you couldn't extinguish with handcuffs, jail, or deportation. They would stand up in court and admit everything, sending a message to the whole country. Only Axel looked as if he had lost something that had nothing to do with Christmas or his sister's dollhouse. Perhaps it was a kind of innocence, a purity he'd kept intact and now must live without. Lars met Gunnar's eyes. His brother winked encouragingly. The kind, loyal Gunnar was back. Most important of all, the forgiving Gunnar.

Suckerfish turned up. He walked over to them with a long, measured stride. Very likely he'd been rehearsing all night. His hands were behind his back; he walked along the row until he came to Gunnar, where he stopped, staring at him and rocking slightly on the balls of his feet.

"So you see, Gunnar Balstrup, the game is up."

Gunnar stared straight ahead and said, "You're wrong there, Svend Hansen. It's only just begun."

The gestapo man's smug expression threatened to fade. Finally, with a nasty smirk, he took a step back, chuckling. As he did so the gates swung open. A heavy gray-green armored car drove into the yard. Its only windows were two small peepholes in the back, covered by stout iron bars. The sight of the car seemed to restore Svend Hansen's confidence.

He took Gunnar's meerschaum pipe out of his pocket and studied it with satisfaction. The pipe from Viborg, with Blicher's teethmarks on it.

Meanwhile Axel was being bundled into the vehicle. It was Luffe's turn next. Then Lars, and finally Gunnar, who paused on the step into the car and turned to the gestapo man.

"Where did you find it?" he asked.

"In the depot," said Svend Hansen. "On the floor."

The doors of the armored car were closed and locked. Four soldiers sat in the dimly lit interior. Outside, two motorcycles revved up.

Lars sat beside Luffe as they drove by the fjord in the early light of dawn. Opposite them were Gunnar and Axel. They couldn't see anything. The vehicle had terrible springs and moved slowly and heavily.

Axel looked down at his hands. Lars felt sorry for him. His little sister Agnes would get her beautiful dollhouse tomorrow, but the generous creator himself wouldn't be there. Maybe he was thinking of that.

Lars thought, very briefly, of his parents at home in the rectory. He saw them on the lawn. Oddly enough, it was summer: The sun was shining, the washing was blowing in the wind, the flag was hoisted. They were standing together as if posing for a photograph, one that would be framed and saved.

Several other pictures flashed before him. Rosen the organist in his little room, in front of the wall containing the watercolors from Hildesheim. The pictures sent by a woman called Nina. Was Nina still alive? Was Filip Rosen alive? Then a picture he would never forget, of a snowman in the red sunset and Irene on the left, looking straight into his lens, her face empty of expression.

Lars closed his photo album and thought about the principal at school. With luck, the principal would light a candle for them.

"I knew there was something I'd overlooked," muttered

Gunnar. "But I thought I'd mislaid my pipe in the loft or the sacristy. Or maybe over at your place, Luffe."

Axel said they were leaving town; he could tell from the sound.

Leaving town. It had such a final ring to it. Lars pictured the globe on his desk, its countries, continents, and oceans spinning around and around.

At that moment they heard three hoots out on the fjord.

A familiar sound—the little ferry hooting. Yet today it was entirely different.

Lars looked up and met Gunnar's eyes.

The three hoots sounded again. A signal. A message to the town, to the Germans, but most of all to the four of them in the prison van.

Three triumphant notes. Otto! He'd managed to get away! He was free.

Gunnar's face seemed to glow from within. A happy, thankful smile spread across his features. Luffe put his head back and roared with laughter. Even Axel cheered up and started rocking jubilantly back and forth.

"Otto," whispered Gunnar, much moved. "You did it, Otto!"

Luffe began stamping on the floor of the vehicle, and he and Gunnar swayed in unison. Luffe had tears in his eyes. Axel and Lars fell into the rhythm of it too. Gunnar and Luffe gazed excitedly at each other as they went to work on their old jingle, loud, plain, and clear.

Lars leaned his head against the side of the vehicle and

closed his eyes. His lips shaped the words of the rhyme about the four Nazi swine, but in his mind's eye, yet again, he saw the picture of a carefree boy pulling a rowboat through shallow water as he looked for mussels. On a summer's day in Denmark.